GUNS OF THE LAWLESS

GUNS OF THE LAWLESS

Todhunter Ballard

SAGEBRUSH
Large Print Westerns

First published in Great Britain by Gunsmoke
First published in the United States by Popular Library

Published in Large Print 2009 by ISIS Publishing Ltd.,
7 Centremead, Osney Mead, Oxford OX2 0ES
United Kingdom
by arrangement with
Golden West Literary Agency

British Library Cataloguing in Publication Data
Ballard, Todhunter, 1903–1980.
    Guns of the lawless
    1. Western stories.
    2. Large type books.
    I. Title
    813.5'2–dc22

ISBN 978–0–7531–8258–1 (hb)

Printed and bound in Great Britain by
T. J. International Ltd., Padstow, Cornwall

CHAPTER
ONE

The grinding of dry brake shoes on iron wheels woke Vance Clark from his doze, and he stood up stiffly, glad to break contact with the soiled cane seat. He reached down his small hand grip from the overhead rack as the coach door opened to admit the rumbling of the train, and the uniformed brakeman sent his nasal call of "Elkhead! Elkhead!" ringing through the smoke-filled car.

Clark lurched along the littered aisle toward the head of the coach, passing a dozen sleepers who stirred protestingly as the brakes jerked down the pace of the train. He pulled the door inward and came onto the welcome freshness of the open platform.

The wind, blowing directly from the distant Sawtooth range, brought with it the smell of pluming smoke from the panting engine and a chill which made Clark shiver inside his sheepskin-lined coat.

He was a big man, his height emphasized by his bell-crowned hat, and his face looked gaunt and drawn. Although he was coming home a winner, he had no sense of accomplishment. He knew that no matter what the court said, the battle had not yet started.

He frowned at the dark stock pens as the train slid by, and at the lights which flicked out of the desert night to form the pattern of the town.

The train was coasting now, coming in beside the edge of the level platform, hissing for its stop beside the yellow station with its single signal standard.

His coach drew up exactly opposite the bell window, behind which he could see the telegraph instrument and the green shaded lamp He dropped to the platform before the wheels lost the last of their momentum. He stood motionless, his back to the train, his quick eyes taking in every detail before him. He saw Roy Hunter, the agent, step out to meet the conductor, his hand filled with orders, and then he saw Bryce Austin descend the steps of the train's only sleeping car and walked toward him across the scarred boards.

At once some of the tension flowed out of him, and he moved ahead so that they met where the yellow light flowed from the station window to lay a band of gold across their path.

For a wordless instant they stopped, staring at each other, two men with hate ingrained, a hate which festered and increased like pus oozing from a broken sore.

Then the lawyer turned away, his long legs carrying him across the trampled surface of the station yard and up the length of Elkhead's main street.

He was barely gone before Joe Spain rounded the far corner of the baggage room, materializing from the darkness like a bandy-legged gnome, a little man with a thin, intent face and hair so light flaxen that he might have been an albino.

Watching, Clark had the feeling that Spain had waited purposely until the lawyer had passed, and the corners of his mobile mouth quirked inward with displeasure that any rider from the Rocking Chair should deliberately avoid a meeting with any man.

Spain came toward him with his horseman's gait, his hundred-pound body bending a little as if the downdraft from the distant hills threatened to carry him away. He stopped, giving Clark a tight grin and saying in a dry, rustling voice,

"Your train was a good two hours late."

He had been drinking. The smell of the sour mash whiskey was heavy upon him, and Clark threw him a troubled look, knowing Spain's deep weakness. But the man was near sober, and this, coupled with his action in staying out of Bryce Austin's sight, told plainer than any words the strain under which he labored.

He nodded. "Who's in town?"

"Munger, with a sore head and a full crew, acting as if someone stole his bear."

"Where?"

"The Palace."

"Let's go."

Worry built up in the thin face of the small man, and embarrassment which was not normal roughened his voice.

"Gilbert said no. Gilbert wants you to come straight to the ranch."

3

Vance Clark did not appear to hear. He repeated, "Let's go," and swung around to follow the way Bryce Austin had taken across the railroad yard to the foot of the town's street, walking so rapidly that the protesting Spain was forced into a half trot to keep pace.

Behind them the train was preparing to depart, steam spitting from the connections as the throttle eased back and the light drivers spun on the smooth track. The smoke poured from the bell stack and the five cars started with a coupling jerk that could be heard for a long mile.

Ahead of them Elkhead's main street was a crazy quilt of shadow and light, the light coming from the windows of half a dozen saloons, the livery, the Chinese restaurant and the frame hotel.

They reached the end of the board sidewalk and moved on to the shadowed hotel porch. There they paused, for someone had called Vance Clark's name from the darkness. Heels tapped across the hollow boards of the gallery, and Virginia Munger stood above them.

She said to Spain in a sharp, commanding tone, "Move on, Joe, wait at the livery," and after a single questioning glance the little rider obeyed.

Then to Vance Clark she said quickly, "Father's in town."

"Joe told me. I rather expected him to be."

"He brought Ernie and five of the boys. He's mad."

"I rather expected that too."

"Don't see him tonight, please."

He made a half turn, peering through the gloom. He could not see her clearly, but he did not need to. Her image was engraved on his memory.

This was a blue-eyed girl, with fair hair which held its natural curl, a laughing girl, reckless in her own way. Yet even in the days gone by, when all of them had been much younger, there had been a steadiness about her which belied her youth.

He said flatly, "I won't run, Ginny."

An edge of urgency crept into her tone. "No one wants you to run, Vance. Just use a little sense. You whipped my father in court, and Petry is not one to take a beating easily."

Vance Clark's voice was soft. "It's something he has yet to learn."

"He'll never learn that," she said, and both of them knew she spoke the truth.

"He'll have to." There was a stubbornness in Vance Clark, and a basic honesty which held him to a purpose once taken even though his intuition told him that his task was impossible.

"I hate to see trouble between you two." She had moved down the steps until only a foot separated them in the night's darkness.

Her very presence shook him as nothing ever had. It seemed to him that this had been true always, almost since their first meeting so long ago.

But he schooled himself as he had schooled himself for years, saying only, "The trouble is not of my making."

That also was true. The trouble was not of his making. Yet in a sense he was the whole pivot point of the argument, for without him Gilbert Grover would have lacked the courage to carry on the fight.

The country knew this, and Petry Munger knew this, and Petry Munger hated him accordingly. It was, Vance thought, a curious facet of human nature that a man should misjudge the reactions of another and hate the misjudged one for his own mistake.

When Petry Munger had decided to split the ranch, to take his share and quit his partnership with Gilbert Grover, it had not occurred to him that Vance Clark would stay with Grover.

Munger had nothing but contempt for his former partner, and he had assumed in his arrogant way that all the world would share that contempt.

He was a ruthless man, a cunning, unscrupulous man. Starting with nothing but a horse, he had worked his way up during twenty-five years from a drifting rider to the foremanship and then a partnership in the huge Rocking Chair ranch.

To most people that would have been enough, but to Munger with his spreading dreams it was only a beginning. He had startled the valley and the country around it six months ago by demanding that his partner sell out to him.

The ultimatum, for it was nothing less, had shocked Gilbert Grover, lost as he was in his bird collection, his interest in rocks and his long, sequestered hours of reading.

For years the day-by-day management of the ranch had been in Munger's hands. It was he who decided what stock to sell, what range to save for winter feed. He dominated the crew and the country, and in a sense the state, and on the night when the showdown came, he had dominated Grover's room.

Vance Clark would never forget that night if he lived to be a hundred. Summoned from the bunkhouse at midnight by the old cook, with sleep still clogging his brain, he had walked up through the powder of snow covering the yard and come into the big room at the front of the old house. Gilbert Grover had been a sunken figure deep in the chair behind the desk, with Munger standing over him.

Munger spoke as he came in.

"We've split the ranch," Munger said. "I offered to buy out the old fool and he refused. I'm taking all the stock south of the Stinking Water, he can have what is to the north. At daybreak you and the crew start venting the brands. Use a double M. I'll have it registered as soon as I can."

Vance Clark turned to the man behind the desk. Gilbert Grover was the only father he had ever known, and he gave Grover a strong, continuing loyalty which had never been put into words.

"What about it?" he said.

Grover made a tired gesture with his thin hand. "I can't hold a man who doesn't want to stay, but I'd rather hoped you would see your way clear to side with me."

"Of course," Vance Clark said.

Some instinct prompted him to watch Petry Munger as he said it. He saw the man's face swell.

Munger said thickly, "You're not a fool, Vance."

"Maybe."

"Without me this ranch won't last six months."

Vance said nothing.

"I taught you everything you know. I took you as a ragtailed kid and made a rider out of you."

This much Vance would not deny. Munger had schooled him. But it was Grover who had given him kindness and sympathy and understanding.

"I stay with Gilbert," he said, and left the room.

All this ran through the filter of his mind now, as he stood facing Virginia Munger, and with it the bitter knowledge that the trouble had built a wall between them which could not be breached. He heard her sigh, and knew that if she had asked anything else of him he would do it gladly. But this was a fight, and in it he could show no willingness to compromise for it would be taken as a sign of weakness.

"It's no use." The words were a murmur on her lips, yet they reached him clearly.

"No use," he said and swung away, not saying goodbye, knowing that she watched him through the darkness until he reached the door of the livery. There was something final in the parting, a door closed which was not apt to be reopened, and a sadness ran through him, a nostalgic mourning for things past, for pleasant memories.

CHAPTER
TWO

He came into the Palace, knocking aside the batwing doors with more abruptness than necessary, and stood there letting his eyes adjust to the yellow light which the three swinging lamps threw across the long room.

A dozen men were lined up along the bar, and in their middle he made out the burly figure of Petry Munger, between Ernie Sylvester his foreman, and Bryce Austin.

Eight to one. Nice odds, he thought, and moved easily forward to elbow his way into a small space between Ernie Sylvester and the man next to him.

The Double M foreman was short and wiry and redheaded, and his green eyes had a hot intemperence as he turned on Vance Clark.

"Watch your elbows, Vance," he said in a ragged voice. "They're sharp."

Vance Clark's answer was even and unhurried and spaced, a murmur which somehow carried the length of the room.

"Not half as sharp as they will be, Ernie."

They faced each other with no liking. They had shared the same bunkhouse for three years, and as riding boss he had given Sylvester orders which the redhead had resented.

"A big man, in court," Ernie said, and deliberately turned his back. Vance lifted his gaze above Ernie's head and met the black eyes of Petry Munger.

"You've come to celebrate, Vance?"

Vance Clark took time to pour his drink and raise it slowly. "You know me better than that, Petry. I never celebrate until a fight is won."

"You and your courts."

"Not my courts." Vance put his empty glass quietly on the bar and laid a dollar beside it. "You were the one who asked legal advice, Petry. I could have told you it wouldn't work." He shifted his attention then, and had a full look at Bryce Austin's face and saw it redden under the heavy tan, and wanted suddenly to laugh and didn't. "Stinking Water belongs to Rocking Chair. It always has and it always will."

"If you can hold it."

"We'll hold it," he said. "I came in here to give you a warning. Move your cattle out, Petry. Move them tomorrow or we'll push them into the sink."

A high, wild anger suddenly gripped Petry Munger. It seemed to paralyze his vocal muscles and make speech impossible. He choked as if gasping for breath, and then he said in a voice so hoarse that it was hard to understand, "I'll hang the first man I catch with a Double M cow."

"Not if the cow is on our land," Vance said. "Or I'll have you in the courts again, and this time it will take more than a scheming lawyer to get you out."

Bryce Austin came away from the bar in a little rush, his lips tight, his gray eyes dangerous.

"I've stood enough of your remarks, Vance."

He waited then, as if certain that Clark would make the first move, as if he wanted Clark to make the first move. Vance stood perfectly quiet, studying the lawyer.

This, he thought was a fleeting bitterness, was the man Virginia Munger had chosen to marry. On the face of it her choice was understandable. Austin had what so few in this wild country possessed — education and background and the social graces.

A handsome man, he had made no secret of his past, of the constant trouble he had been in during his school years, of the fact that a wealthy family had more or less exiled him to this desert land.

He was still only in his late twenties, and the whisper of wildness lent him a certain dash, a mysterious quality which many people found interesting. And certainly, since coming to Elkhead, Bryce Austin had seemingly changed. Already he was the district's leading attorney, and Vance more than half suspected that Austin had pushed Petry Munger into making his open break with Grover; that Austin was already setting up his future father-in-law as the state's most powerful man.

But at the trial over the Stinking Water he had discovered an unexpected weakness in Austin. The man was vain. He could not stand needling and he could not stand to lose. His loss of the water case had enraged Austin and they had almost come to blows in the corridor outside the state court. If the judge himself had not happened by there would have been a fight.

But there was no judge in this saloon. Vance Clark was alone, outnumbered eight to one. The burning, hungry desire in the lawyer's eyes could be answered in only one way.

"All right," Clark said, and saw Austin's overhand blow start. He ducked under it, felt the heavy forearm as it struck across his shoulder, and buried his own fist in the man's stomach.

Now, the fight started, he knew that it had been inevitable since that first dance when Virginia Munger had met the lawyer. He recalled his jealousy then, as he stood against the rough schoolhouse wall flanked by a group of riders, and watched the laughing girl whirl lightly in Austin's arms.

He felt the man before him bend under the force of his blow, and heard the air whistle from the lawyer's throat. He stepped back, swinging a curving hook which caught Austin along the line of his jaw. He took a left to the head and a right which struck solidly against the side of his neck.

They lost all science then, each seeming to know instinctively that this was a battle without rules. They stood and slugged toe to toe, two big men, young men, their muscles hard and resilient.

They fought on, and no one interfered. The men along the bar might be hostile to the Rocking Chair but there was not one among them, Petry Munger included, who did not enjoy the fight.

12

A fist came out of nowhere and smashed into Vance Clark's eye. He chopped at the lawyer's chin and missed, and their arms went about each other. They stood struggling for an instant and then went to the dirty floor together, crashing against a table, bringing it down with their fall. They rolled over and over, until Austin's head cracked against the corner of the bar and his grip relaxed.

Vance Clark struggled to his feet, wiping his mouth with the back of his hand. He stared at the blood streak across his bronzed skin which his bruised lips left, then he turned and started unseeingly for the door.

Behind him Ernie Sylvester said, "Wait a minute, Vance."

He turned slowly, wearily. It had been a long, hard day, and the lawyer's fists had found him many times. He saw the redheaded foreman through puffed eyes, saw his mocking smile, heard him say,

"Your fight isn't over yet, friend Vance."

He looked slowly around then, at the row of grinning faces, and he could see what was in their minds. It would be Sylvester next, and if he whipped the foreman, someone else. The Double M had suffered a blow to its pride, and it meant for him to pay. He knew now that they never expected him to walk from this saloon, that he would be beaten until he could not stand.

He paused, his legs trembling a little from sheer weariness, and looked into Sylvester's mocking eyes. He had a gun in his holster, and he knew that Sylvester wanted him to draw. They all wanted him to draw.

13

He did not believe this had been rehearsed, but it could not have played more perfectly into the hands of the Double M if they had gone over each part of the action in advance.

Beaten as he was, he could not possibly pull his gun faster than Sylvester could, and he had seen the redheaded man shoot, many times.

He ran his tongue around his bleeding lips, tasting the salty flavor of the blood, trying to clear his head, his eyes ranging along the line of men before the bar.

They returned his look eagerly, challengingly. It was a trap and he was nicely within its jaws, and there seemed no escape. And then, as Sylvester moved a step forward, made reckless by his desire, Joe Spain's dry voice came from the saloon's rear door.

"Easy does it, Ernie."

For an instant every man in the room was frozen, and in the resulting deep silence Bryce Austin groaned and stirred and tried to sit up.

Vance Clark realized with a start that he had forgotten the lawyer, that they had all forgotten Austin in their sharp attention to the scene being played.

"Don't move." Joe Spain stepped into the room. His eyes were bright, and the guns in his small hands looked very large. "Don't move, Ernie."

Sylvester did not move. No one along the bar moved. They stood rigid, disbelieving, the eagerness dying out of their faces, giving way to growing rage.

Petry Munger said harshly, "I won't forget this, Joe."

"Why," Joe Spain said, "I don't know that I want you to. Get their guns, Vance."

14

Clark got their guns. It made quite an arsenal, once he had them all collected. He nodded at the watching bartender, who had kept well out of the fight.

"A sack."

The man found a sack and Clark dumped the captured arms into it. Bryce Austin climbed shakily to his feet, using the corner of the bar as a ladder to raise himself. He watched with dull, angry eyes. Petry Munger held the cold butt of a cigar in one side of his tight-lipped mouth.

"This doesn't finish it, Vance."

Vance Clark thought tiredly that nothing was ever finished. He picked up the sack, throwing it over his shoulder. "I'll drop these at the livery."

No one spoke. He nodded to Joe Spain and they moved toward the batwing doors. Behind them the long room was blanketed in explosive silence.

Outside on the street they walked side by side toward the livery. Joe Spain was chuckling under his breath.

"I been wanting to do that for years — throw a gun on Petry Munger. Did you see his face?"

Vance Clark did not answer. As they passed the hotel he caught a glimpse of a white dress far back in the shadows. His impulse was to stop, but something kept him moving ahead. It would not be long before Virginia Munger learned that twice within this day he had whipped the man she was going to marry, once with his fists and once in the courtroom at the distant state house. Again he experienced no feeling of satisfaction, but only a deepening sense of loss.

CHAPTER
THREE

The home ranch of the Rocking Chair was in the mouth of a canyon where a small stream coming from springs halfway up the mountain brought its fresh water tumbling down the narrow cleft.

The yard was big, the sheds and corral and bunkhouses in good repair. Once this had been almost a settlement within itself, two houses standing on opposite sides of the creek, one occupied by Gilbert Grover and his daughter, the other by Munger and Virginia.

But now the Munger house stood dark and deserted, a silent reminder that the Rocking Chair was split, and that Petry Munger's bull-like voice would no longer sound across the yard.

Two hours after midnight, Vance Clark and Joe Spain walked their tired horses into the yard. A light still burned in Gilbert Grover's office. Vance sighed and stepped from the saddle. Turning his horse over to Spain, he ambled wearily across the hard-baked earth to the long, shadowed porch.

He came into the central hall without knocking, and sent his low call running through the house. "Anybody up?"

At once the office door opened and he saw Judy framed in the panel of light. She was a small girl, dark where Virginia Munger was fair, intense where Virginia was relaxed.

"Vance." She came toward him, moving with quick, nervous energy. "We'd about given you up."

"The train was late." He walked on toward the door, dreading to step into the light, dreading for them to see the marks of the fight upon his face.

She backed away, giving him passage, and he came into the familiar room to see Gilbert Grover behind his desk. This room had never seemed to be part of the ranch. Its walls were hidden by glass cabinets whose shelves held a huge collection of mounted birds.

Those cases contained specimens of almost every type of bird to be found in that part of the country and many which were entirely foreign to the desert. The man in the chair was nearly as foreign to the land as was his collection. He was small, with a tiny bone frame which his daughter had inherited. But here the resemblance ceased, for Judy flowed with boundless energy while Gilbert Grover was one of the quietest men Clark had ever known.

Looking at him in this moment Clark again had the feeling that Grover did not belong here. His life should have been spent within the sheltering walls of some museum, where he could pursue his hobby untroubled by the roughshod cares of a workaday world.

That he had inherited the Rocking Chair from his father was one of the tricks of fate sometimes played on the inoffensive man. That he realized he was unqualified by either aptitude or temperament to run the big ranch properly spoke for his awareness, and that he had had sense enough to pick Petry Munger out of the crew and make him first the foreman and then a partner showed that he was a good judge of ability.

But his judgment failed in the last analysis, for he had underestimated the extent of Petry Munger's ambition. It had never occurred to him that Munger might reach a point where he would want the whole ranch. And when Munger pulled out it had been a heavy blow to Gilbert Grover's frail spirit.

He said now in his gentle voice, "Welcome home, Vance," and stared at the red welts, the discolored eye and the cut lip which were Vance Clark's souvenirs of the fight.

"What happened?"

Clark dropped his bag beside the door and walked over to the desk, the student lamp throwing his shadow long and grotesque across the floor and up the specimen case against the far wall. He glanced at it and met the glassy stare of a horned owl.

"You got my wire?"

Gilbert Grover nodded. "I judge the court decided in our favor."

"They did. My train was late and when I stepped into the Palace, Munger was there, with Ernie Sylvester and half their crew."

"Who marked you — Munger?"

"Austin. He didn't like the way the case went and he didn't like some of the remarks I made."

18

From behind him Judy laughed, a high, bubbling sound.

"I'll bet he didn't. Mr. Stuffed Shirt Austin takes himself too seriously to like anything anyone says except himself."

Behind the desk Gilbert Grover made an unhappy murmur. "I never trusted Austin." He said this as much to himself as to the others in the room. "He was a little too sure of himself for my taste, and I'll always feel that if he hadn't put ideas into Petry Munger's head none of this trouble would have started."

To a certain extent Vance Clark agreed. But Petry Munger had always had ideas, and the break would have come sooner or later even if Bryce Austin had not showed up in the country.

"So we won," Gilbert said, still speaking half to himself.

"We won," Vance Clark said. "At least the court ruled that none of the land holdings including the water rights to the Stinking Water were ever included in the partnership agreement. That's what Judge Tyler thought when I first discussed the case with him. He drew up the original agreement, and it dealt with cattle only. Austin's contention in court was that his client had been cheated — that Munger believed he owned a full partnership in the ranch, land and water rights as well as cattle."

"He knew better," Grover said. "At the time I decided to take him into partnership he had a small herd of cattle which he had been running with our animals. I told him that if he would throw in his cattle and take over active management of the ranch we'd split even on all the increase."

He was silent, thinking. "This trouble is partly my fault, however. I'll admit that for ten years I've paid very little attention to ranch affairs."

Clark knew that he hadn't, and that Gilbert knew he knew it, and out of his impatience came a rather sharp retort. "Let's not worry about that now. Let's worry about what we're going to do."

Gilbert Grover's eyes behind his square steel-rimmed glasses opened wider. "Do? But you said that we'd won."

Clark wanted to sit down. Waves of tiredness ran up through his big body. "I said," he corrected, "that the court ruled that the deeded land and the water rights are yours. I didn't say we were out of trouble. We'll never be as long as Petry Munger has the strength to push a cow onto our grass."

Both Grover and the girl stared at him in tight silence.

"But they can't. If the law says the land is ours —"

Vance Clark lost his remaining patience. Gilbert Grover was not as stupid as he was making himself appear. Grover just dreaded the fight ahead. He was trying to convince himself that he had nothing to worry about. Like an ostrich, he was hiding from his enemies by burying his head in the sand.

He said sharply, "As long as Petry Munger ran the Rocking Chair he ran this country with a high hand. You know that."

Grover made a little disparaging gesture. Clark paid no attention. "And he won't change now that he's running a brand of his own. He'll claim he was cheated out of his rights by a crooked court, and half the people in the country will sympathize with him. The Rocking Chair isn't well liked, Gilbert. No big outfit that dominates a country is well liked by the little fellows who surround it. Most of them hate the brand, and they'll forget that it was Petry Munger who made them hate it. They'll only recall that Munger has now suffered too at the hands of the ranch. They'll be on his side."

He sensed that Judy was watching him carefully, weighing every word he said, and he threw a glance at the girl. Her small face had a tight, set look about it and he saw none of the softness there, none of the indecision which marked her father. Judy had a mind of her own. She always knew what she wanted, and she always went after it.

"But what can Petry do?"

"There are many things he can do," Clark said grimly. "When he left he took most of the crew with him. Many of them are men he hired, men who owe their loyalty to him rather than to the ranch. He owns half the cows. His animals all wear the Rocking Chair brand and have been vented with the Double M. What's to keep him from going on branding? Branding your half of the stock, stealing you blind? All he has to do is change the brand and we couldn't prove whether an animal belonged to his original half or not."

Gilbert Grover stared at him, horror-struck. "Surely you don't think Petry Munger would steal my cattle? Why — why, I've known him for over twenty years. He was my partner for more than ten."

Privately Vance Clark believed that there were few things in the world Petry Munger would not try if he thought he was being blocked in his aims. He said aloud,

"He'll talk himself into it. Right now he probably figures he was robbed in court, and Petry isn't a man to take being robbed lying down. So his next step is to try to pay himself back by rebranding your cows — and the hell of it is, we haven't got enough men to watch him. You might say we haven't any men at all."

Gilbert Grover worried his lower lip with his teeth. "Maybe I should see him. Maybe if I offered to sell him the Stinking Water he'd be satisfied."

Vance Clark was too tired to argue. He turned, saying across his shoulder, "There's nothing more we can do tonight. I'll get some sleep." He stepped out into the hall, knowing as he did so that the man at the desk was glad to see him go, that Gilbert Grover never made a decision today that he could put off until the morrow.

But he counted without Judy. She followed him into the hall.

"You forgot your bag."

He took it from her, and she noted the tired lines of his face and the dark circles under his eyes. "Some coffee?"

He said, "Nothing but sleep, kid," and squeezed her arm. They had grown up together, and his feeling for

22

this small girl was the same as if she were a younger sister.

But she was not satisfied. She followed him onto the dark porch. "You think it will be bad, Vance?"

"You know Petry as well as I do."

She nodded, the motion of her shoulders showing faintly in the half light. "I know, and Dad is no fighter. He'd rather spend his time skinning and stuffing his silly birds." There was a note of discontent in her tone which he had never heard there before.

"Easy, kid." He would have moved away but again she stopped him. "Tell me something, Vance. I know that when the split came Petry offered you the foreman's job with the new outfit. You knew what father is like. You knew that if you stayed the fight would rest on your shoulders, that without you there would be no fight, that Dad would lie down and let them march over him."

"I guess so."

"Then why did you stay?"

He leaned a shoulder point against one of the porch posts, looking out across the dark yard, trying to put into words something which he had never clearly thought through for himself.

"This is the only home I ever had," he said. "I came here from Texas with my brother, a rag-tailed kid, and my brother got himself killed in a saloon brawl. I don't know what would have happened to me if the crew hadn't picked me up and hauled me out here."

She said, "That doesn't answer my question, Vance. You were raised here, yes. But Petry had more to do with it than my father did."

He looked down at her face, a pale triangle in the dimness. "In a way, yes." He was not a man who talked often or easily. His thoughts grew inward, protected by a natural reserve, by a fear of being hurt. "But there was no kindness in Petry, not even for Virginia. He treated me for exactly what I was, a helper, a kid too young to draw a man's wages. Your father was different. Your father knew that a boy needed something of life besides food and work. He saw that I went to school with you and Virginia, that I had books to read, that I knew there was another world outside of the sand flats and desert sinks of this country. He was kind and I loved him, and I love him still."

She said, "I see."

He wondered how much she did see. They had grown up together, he and the two girls, playing together, dancing together, riding together. And always with him, from the very first, it had been Virginia. It was something over which he had no conscious control, something that during their early years he himself had hardly noticed. It had always been Virginia Munger, it always would be, and nothing that had happened on this night or on any other night would ever change it.

The bunkhouse was cold, and had a deserted feel. Once it had housed ten men, had rung with their horseplay and their laughter. But now only he and Joe Spain remained.

He undressed in the darkness and settled exhaustedly into his blankets. He was very tired, but an unreasoning restlessness kept sleep away. He lay there trying to plan the morrow and having no ideas.

24

They had won their case in court, and before the law the title to the owned acres belonged to Gilbert Grover. But this was a remote land, a land of fiercely burning desert sinks, of dry lakes whose blowing surfaces had not seen rain in fifty years. Only in the mountains and on the benches was there sufficient moisture for grass to grow, for cattle to live and feed.

It was these springs which Gilbert Grover owned, these swiftly running streams which hurried their way down the side canyons to lose their moisture in the hungry sands below. If they could hold these springs they would hold the land, for the five million acres of public graze was useless without them.

But he had no illusion about Petry Munger. Petry had cattle, and Petry had to have Rocking Chair water for those cattle to live. What he needed he would take. Of that much Vance Clark was certain.

This certainty brought him out of his blankets before full light. He shook out Joe Spain, ignoring the small man's grumbling protests, and sent him to saddle the horses while he went to rouse the cook.

They breakfasted in silence and rode out of the yard before the sun topped the eatern horizon. They rode steadily, on a familiar trail that lifted up onto the shoulder of the bench and skirted the mountain on their right to come around the resulting elbow toward the Stinking Water line camp forty miles away.

This was a country of sharp contrasts, as if nature had amused herself in putting it together. Mountains are seldom single rises but rather individual upthrusts from a central chain, yet here each mountain stood alone, rising out of the great Nevada plain, separated from its fellows by sandy wastes too vast to be seen across.

The Rocking Chair range had consisted of two such mountains, each lifting a good three thousand feet above the mile-high plain, with fifty miles of dry lake between them.

In the old days before Grover and Munger split, the range had been divided into two equal parts, as nature intended. The home ranch sprawled at the foot of North Mountain, as they called the huge swelling of rock where Bander Creek dashed out of the higher canyon to give him water and grass.

On the sink side, hot springs spewed a thousand gallons an hour into the small, man-made lake which had been created by throwing an earth dam across the canyon's mouth, and from this lake ran a ditch, to water the spreading hay fields that supplied the ranch's winter feed.

In summer the stock ranged high on the mountainsides, climbing slowly as the snow line receded and the lower springs began to dry, but with the coming of winter storms they were worked down again to the lower benches now watered by the seasonal rains, until the snow heaped deep enough to make feeding necessary.

In a sense, therefore, the Stinking Water line camp was far more the true center of the ranch than were the home buildings, and Vance Clark headed toward it, guessing that this would be the point at which Petry Munger would strike first.

Joe Spain was never one to talk when words were not essential, and he held his peace until after they had made their dry noon camp and pushed on.

"Gilbert know what you mean to do?" he said finally.

"I don't know myself," Vance said.

Spain considered this in taciturn silence. In another man that silence might have been mistaken for surliness, but Clark had known the small rider for many years. It was only Joe's way of masking worry.

"Seems like," Spain said, "it's time someone found out."

Vance Clark agreed with him thoroughly. It was time that someone found out, time someone came up with a carefully planned program, if they meant to hold Rocking Chair.

He said, "The first thing is to have a look at Stinking Water. The cattle Petry took in the split are all on the South Mountain. He can't cross the sink until fall, but come fall he'll need feed."

The little man nodded.

"It's already haying time. I've got to get a crew out there and cut the stuff or we'll all be out of feed come winter."

Again Joe Spain nodded.

"But I don't want to send a crew out if Petry has already seized the camp."

The smile Spain showed him was a tiny, mocking thing. "And you don't want to stack hay for Petry Munger to grab next winter. It looks to me, friend Vance, like you're between the devil and the mountain. If you don't cut hay we have no winter feed, and if you do Petry drives his stock across the sink after the first storm and we don't have hay anyway."

Clark did not answer. The trail ahead of them looped upward over a rocky shoulder and then down, crossing an arm of sand which ran from the dry lake into a small canyon. They climbed to the next rise and came through brush timber, rounding a craggy promontory.

Below them stretched nearly a thousand acres of level land crosscut by ditches, the waist-high grass showing startling green, like an emerald checkerboard rimmed by the rock and brush of the mounting hillsides.

The sight always brought a lift to Vance Clark. It was a sight which would have pleased any cowman: acres of growing feed, assurance that his herds would not starve in the coming winter months.

But the pleasure lasted a moment only, for the camp which should have been deserted showed activity in the distant yard, and a plume of smoke lifted lazily from the cook house chimney.

Vance Clark hauled up with a whispered oath, and Joe Spain whistled softly through his broken teeth. They sat their horses, studying the scene, trying to guess how many men were holding the camp.

Then without a word Vance turned his horse out of the trail, climbing the rocky shoulder to his left, hearing Joe Spain's mount behind him on the slippery grade.

The country was exceedingly rough. The whole southern face of North Mountain rose abruptly from the sink, cut here and there by small canyons down which wound the cattle tracks. They came into one of these and crossed it. They found their way up the side beyond and crossed a hog-back, dropping downward into a slanting canyon which led west toward the springs above.

As they pushed on the smell of the distant springs rose in a nauseous wave, foul and penetrating. It seemed strange that this water which smelled so bad as it came out of the ground was somehow purified by oxygen as it coursed down the three-mile ditch. By the time it reached the hay camp it had lost most of its odor and was drinkable.

They reached the earth dam, rising for thirty feet above their heads, and followed the flume down through a break in the hills toward the house.

They had almost gained the level ground when a voice from their left called, "Hold up," and they discovered Ernie Sylvester on the rock shoulder above them, a rifle across his knees.

CHAPTER
FOUR

Sylvester stood up slowly. He was a spare man of thirty-five with a narrow face and a pointed nose. His eyes were green and mocking, and his face had a certain cherry redness which some redheads get instead of suntan.

"Riding for fun?"

Vance Clark did not answer. Joe Spain whistled tonelessly through his broken teeth, a habit he had when he was worrying about something. Ernie grinned at him.

"Drop your guns."

They obcycd silcntly, pulling thc hand guns from their holsters and letting them fall to the rocky trail.

"Now your rifles."

They lifted their rifles from the boots. Ernie gathered up the hardware and stacked it on the stone beside the trail. "Now get down, Vance."

Clark dismounted.

"Ride ahead, Joe."

Spain rode. After a moment Vance followed on foot without being told. He sensed rather than saw that behind him Ernie had lifted himself into the saddle and was riding Vance's horse.

They came on down the trail beside the swiftly running water of the ditch, crossing the laterals which spread out like veins in a leaf to irrigate the thick grass.

Unconsciously Vance noticed that the stand of hay was better than he had ever seen it, and thought bitterly that this was the way things usually worked. Petry would get the biggest hay crop in history if he remained in control of Stinking Water.

They trailed into the yard. They saw half a dozen riders loafing before the cook shack and Petry Munger and Bryce Austin standing on the porch. The lawyer's face was puffed with marks of last night's fight, and his eyes narrowed as he recognized Sylvester's prisoners.

Petry Munger showed no surprise. He walked to the edge of the porch and waited for the trio to move up before him, hearing Ernie Sylvester say in his mocking voice,

"Look who I found wandering around loose in the hills. Say hello to Mr. Munger, boys."

Joe Spain checked his horse some six feet from the porch. He sat, crouched a little in the saddle, looking smaller than ever. Instead of speaking, he spat elaborately into the dust.

Petry Munger's face reddened and seemed to swell with anger. The lawyer glowered at the little rider.

The men loafing around the bunkhouse moved forward, expectancy upon their faces. Munger controlled himself with an effort.

"Come on into the house," he told Vance Clark. "I want to talk to you."

Clark stepped past Joe Spain. As he did so their eyes met. Clark shook his head a trifle, then climbed the log steps and went into the house.

The line camp building was old, of adobe, going back to the early sixties when some Mormon had set up a ranch below the hot springs. Later, when Young recalled his faithful to Salt Lake, the Mormon abandoned the place. Still later, it had been filed on by a man named Peters, who built the earth dam and the ditch, setting up a hay ranch which he in turn sold out to Gilbert Grover's father.

The house was not much changed. A Piute and his squaw lived in a small shack below the ditch, the squaw cooking for the haying crew in season and the buck keeping an eye on the fences that held straying cattle out of the hay.

For weeks on end there would be no one else at the camp. It was only after the cattle were brought down for winter feed that a crew was kept here. At other times single line riders patrolling the mountain's foot stopped here occasionally on their lonely rounds.

Dust covered everything. Obviously Munger and his men had only arrived that day, and the absence of blankets or other bedding indicated that Munger had not meant to stay here.

This puzzled Clark but he said easily, "You know you're trespassing, Petry. The court ruled that Stinking Water and the home ranch belong to Gilbert."

Munger grunted. He took a straight chair and turned it, straddling the seat and leaning forward to rest his crossed arms on the top of the chair back.

"I watched you grow up, Vance. I never thought you were a fool."

Vance Clark was used to Petry Munger's peremptory manner. Munger treated most people with unquestioning contempt.

He said in an even voice, "What have I done now that's foolish?"

"Backed a losing game. When I decided to split from Grover I figured that you'd come with me, that you would be my foreman."

"So I understood."

Again Munger's face seemed to swell, and again he controlled himself.

"But instead you stayed with Gilbert."

Clark knew he could explain the various reasons which had made him remain with the Rocking Chair rather than pull away with the Double M, but he also knew that none of his reasons would appear valid in the older man's eyes.

Munger was a pirate, a buccaneer who had met life squarely and taken what he wanted from it. The one thing he could not comprehend was weakness, and Gilbert Grover was weak. He had split with Grover as soon as he reached the point where he no longer needed Grover's name and his backing and his credit, and he would despoil Grover as ruthlessly as he would have despoiled a small nester foolhardy enough to settle on his range.

So Clark said nothing.

Munger's voice turned bitter. "If you hadn't been there, pushing him, Grover would never have had the guts to fight me in court."

Still Vance remained silent, but he realized now that Munger felt he had been betrayed, that Vance Clark had betrayed him by daring to fight him, and his lips tightened.

"Well —" The older man spread his hands. "You won your court battle, but it will do you no good and it will do Grover no good. I'm here at Stinking Water and I'm going to stay. I'll make my headquarters here. I'll run my cattle on South Mountain all this summer and I'll bring them across the sink in the fall. You can keep your part of North Mountain, but make sure your beef doesn't stray onto any of my ground."

Vance said quietly, "I might point out to you that Stinking Water isn't yours, by order of the court."

For the first time since they had entered the room Munger laughed. "Vance, you are a fool after all. I never really thought so before. I watched you grow up. I watched Gilbert stuff your head with all that manure from books, and at one time I thought you were very smart. But I was wrong and Bryce Austin was right. He said you were nothing but an ignorant rider spoiled by a little learning. Let me show you something." He reached for a large roll of paper standing against the wall, and spread it on the table. Vance saw that a rough map had been drawn in ink.

"Here." Munger pointed with his stubby forefinger. "Here are the springs." He indicated the hot springs three miles above. "Here is the house," he indicated another dot, "and the hay fields." His finger rubbed over the space surrounding the dot.

"Now, when Peters filed on this place he filed on half a section, on three hundred and twenty acres, and naturally he filed on the land around the springs. Oh, he owned them all right, and he sold them to Gilbert and Gilbert owns them. No question about that. But these buildings aren't on that half section, nor are most of the hay fields."

Vance Clark felt his stomach knotting.

"So," Munger said, and straightened, "one of my men has filed on these buildings, and another has filed on the lower hay fields, on every inch of grass that Gilbert doesn't already own."

He watched Clark with the pleased expression of a cat about to pounce on a mouse. "That isn't all, friend Vance. Ernie Sylvester has filed on the canyon above the hot springs, and that's the only way down off the mountain for the cattle on this side. We're starting to string fence tomorrow. Rocking Chair cattle are not going to be able to get to Stinking Water unless they cross our property, and they're not going to cross."

Vance heard the words and still did not lift his head. He thought bitterly, Petry licked me. I might have known he would. He's always won. And last night I was so proud of myself, I'd saved Gilbert's springs for him. He owns his springs, and what good will they do him now? He can't get his stock down to the water, or the hay, and most of that is no longer his anyway.

He looked up slowly, none of his conflicting emotions showing in the even mask of his face. "All right. You've got the hay and you've cut us off the springs. But you haven't any water yourself."

Munger laughed again. "You're right, assuming that you divert the flow away from the ditch."

"That's exactly what I intend to do," Vance Clark said grimly.

Munger shrugged. "You can't get to your property without crossing land we hold, and we'll try to see that you don't cross. Also, the hay is ready to cut. I'm bringing in a crew tomorrow morning. We don't need any more water this season for hay, and after the first winter storms enough water falls to take care of the cattle I bring over. By that time I think Gilbert Grover will be ready to sell the springs to me at my price."

"Not if I have anything to say about it."

"I don't believe you will," Petry Munger said. "I have a hunch you'll be out of the country by then, or dead. I called you in here to give you one last chance, and to do Grover a favor at the same time. If you'll ride back to Rocking Chair and tell him how things are, and advise him to sell me Stinking Water, there's a place for you at the Double M."

"And if I don't?"

Petry Munger seemed to be considering. "If you don't, a couple of my boys are going to take you out to the center of the dry lake and put you afoot. It won't be bad tonight. You can walk probably ten or twelve miles before daylight, but once the sun comes up I doubt that you'll ever make it across."

Vance Clark looked at him in disbelief. He had been across the dry lake some twenty times, but always in the fall or spring, after the rains had filled the hollows to furnish water for the passage.

At this time of the year the temperature on the baked sand was well over a hundred, and there was not a drop of water between the Stinking Springs and the South Mountain. A man on a horse would have small chance of survival during the daylight hours. A man on foot would have almost no chance at all.

Munger's heavy face twisted into something he thought was a grin. "I'm bringing a little pressure on you, Vance."

"A little pressure," Vance Clark said.

Before this he had fought for the Rocking Chair because the ranch had been his home, because he had a genuine love for Gilbert Grover, the kind of love some strong men find for the weak. He had been fighting with a throttled anger, directing it more against the lawyer Bryce Austin than against Petry Munger and the crew. But now . . .

"To hell with you," he said, and took one instinctive step forward. If he could reach Petry Munger's thick neck he would choke him. But as he moved, Munger's gun came from its holster, its long barrel trained on Vance's stomach.

Vance Clark saw the gun through a fine red haze. Never in his twenty-five years had he been so angry. His lips were stiff, his words not quite distinct. "Go ahead, shoot me. I'd rather die from a slug than from thirst." He kept walking, slowly, a step at a time. "Go ahead. Shoot."

Munger retreated before him, the gun held level.

"Stop it, Vance. Stop it."

Vance Clark did not stop. He took another step and then another. Munger had backed clear to the far wall. Clark's hands came up and out, his strong fingers curved a little, like claws. Another minute and he would wrap them around Munger's throat.

And then Petry Munger moved with a speed surprising in so big a man. He brought his gun up and down in a swinging slash.

Vance flung his right arm up to block the blow, but Petry Munger had the strength of a bull. The gun barrel crashed down across the center of Vance's head.

Vance went to his knees, driven there by the impact. He was not out, since his raised arm and the crown of his hat had cut some of the force, but the eight-inch barrel of the Frontier Colt was heavy as a section of iron bar. He stayed down, shaking his head in an effort to clear it, his senses slowed as if his mind labored though some thick oily film. The evening gloom in the room seemed to envelop his brain.

Munger stood above him, his face twisted with rage. He said, voice tight in his throat, "You'd have loved for me to shoot you, wouldn't you, Vance? You'd like nothing better than to put Lem Stewart on my tail. Well, you're out of luck. If you die it won't be from my bullet."

He holstered his gun, stooped, and slung Vance Clark's limp body across his own broad shoulder as if

Clark were a sack of flour. Then he wheeled out of the room to the darkening yard beyond.

The crew stood in a half circle with Joe Spain in their midst, surprise blanking their faces as they saw Munger's burden.

Munger dumped Clark on the porch.

"Get his horse and Joe Spain's," he said to Sylvester. "Better tie them to the saddles. Then ride them out to the center of the dry lake and put them afoot."

A wicked pleasure glowed in Sylvester's green eyes as he stared at Vance, slumped on the edge of the steps. Then he swung away through the gathering shadow, nodding to two of the crew. Joe Spain watched him go, and after that he looked up at Petry Munger.

Suddenly the little man moved, wrenching his arms free from the riders who had been holding him carelessly. He grabbed a gun from the belt of the man on his left. He spun away as they tried to grasp him, dropped to one knee and fired at Petry Munger.

The bullet went wide, and the two Double M riders lit on Spain, crushing him beneath their combined weight as they wrestled for the gun.

They got it. They jerked Spain to his feet as Petry Munger came down the steps, all the anger he had felt for Vance Clark redirected toward the little man.

He struck Spain solidly in the face, knocking him to the ground. Spain fell on his back and lay there, stunned, his arms extended. Petry Munger stepped forward deliberately, placing his boot heel on the palm of Spain's right hand. Then he twisted, throwing his whole weight so that the heel bore in, crushing the bones.

Spain cried out highly, sharply, an animal cry without words. It brought Vance Clark from his crouched position in a long leap that carried him to Petry Munger's back. He clung there, wrapping his legs around Munger's thick body as he would ride a bronco, his fingers digging deep into Munger's neck.

Petry tried to shake free, to tear the clutching fingers from his throat. He would not have made it but that two of the crew came to his rescue, dragging Vance Clark off and beating him about the head with their fists.

Vance went down. He lay on the ground, half senseless, yet knowing that somebody was kicking him in the side. Then he felt them lifting him, tying him in the saddle. The horse moved out and he could hear the murmur of the men around him. And after that he felt nothing.

CHAPTER
FIVE

The sun came up over the eastern horizon like a red ball lifting itself from some hidden inferno. Vance Clark turned to squint at it through the slits of his puffed eyes. He had been in fights before. Anyone raised in that bleak country, who had found his pleasure at the Saturday night dances in the scattered schoolhouses, had been in fights. But never in his memory had he been so thoroughly beaten.

His ribs were sore. His head ached, and the puffy cheeks felt as if the skin could no longer stretch enough to cover them. But he was more concerned about Joe Spain than about himself.

The little man's arm hung at his side and the hand was terribly swollen. Even in the best of circumstances they could hardly hope to walk too far without water after the sun came up, and in their present condition there was literally no hope at all.

They would die. The knowledge filled Vance Clark with a surging rebellion. Not that he was afraid of death; he had come close to dying several times in his short life. But he had a burning desire to live, to live at least long enough to settle the score with the men who had put him afoot in this dreary waste.

He walked, one arm under Joe Spain's small shoulders, half supporting the little man's weight, and the bloodless pallor of the weatherstained face told him that Spain could not go much farther.

He faltered now, his legs going rubbery, and said in a stifled voice, "I've gotta sit down."

Vance Clark eased him to the sand, hard-baked as cement. Already the rising sun created heat waves to burn through the thin fabric of his shirt.

He looked back over the long way they had come. Their scuffing feet had left no marks on the dried surface. It was as if they had not passed at all. The country might wonder what had become of them, but before their bodies were apt to be found only bleached bones would be left.

He had found such a pile of bones, long ago, on this lake. Nothing remained to identify their owner save some scraps of metal from his belt fastenings.

"Go on." He realized that Joe Spain was speaking to him, and already the small man's voice sounded something like a croak. "Go on. Without me you might make it."

Vance Clark squatted down at his side. "You don't actually believe that, Joe?"

"No." Joe Spain used his undamaged hand to wipe his lips. "We're not going to make it, Vance. Petry Munger saw to that, damn him."

Vance Clark shrugged. "I'm blaming Austin," he said. "Petry's like a bull-headed animal. He doesn't stop to think or plan, he just goes charging ahead. It was Austin who thought of filing on the hay fields and on the section in the canyon above the Stinking Water."

"Petry put us afoot. Petry ruined my hand, Vance."

Vance Clark turned around slowly. If they could find shelter, any shelter . . . He considered trying to scoop out a hole, to rig their shirts into a kind of canopy, but he had nothing to dig with, nothing he could put up as support for any canopy. And then he saw movement, far off, where the earth seemed to fall away over the horizon.

The dry lake was so large that you could actually see the curvature of the earth where it bent into its great globe, and it was at this point that he thought he saw movement in the west.

Had it been in the east he could have seen nothing, for the glare of the sun's rays would have blinded him, but from the west . . . He watched, afraid to say anything to Joe, afraid to believe his own senses. Later in the day with the sun high he would have been sure that it was a mirage, but now . . . He stood there, straining to see better, almost standing on tip-toe in order to increase his angle of sight.

The distant speck was definite now, like a black pinpoint against the lighter sky. He sat down. He could not bear to watch. The rider, for he judged that it must be a rider, was a good ten miles away.

Joe Spain stirred at his side and groaned, and he looked down at the little man, at that swollen, blackened hand. It made him almost sick. He debated whether to tell Joe about what he had seen. It would give Joe a period of hope — but then, if the rider did not reach them, if no help came, the disappointment might be worse for that very hope.

He stayed silent, but his brain was churning. Perhaps Petry Munger had relented. But he discarded the thought almost as soon as it entered his mind. Petry was not one to relent. He had decided on what to do back at the line camp, and Petry would not change his mind.

Yet one of Petry's riders might. They were hardcases, true enough, but not all of them could be as ruthless as Ernie Sylvester.

He fought to keep from looking at the distant speck. It would take a rider two hours, three hours to reach them, if he was really coming in their direction. It could be someone riding from town, cutting across the lower end of the lake before the heat grew too intense, heading for North Mountain.

He looked. He had no watch, but he judged from the space the sun had climbed in the sky that twenty minutes or half an hour had passed.

As he looked his heart leaped. The black spot was still there, and it seemed larger!

He knew that he could not possibly have seen it at first except for the clear morning air. As the sun climbed the heat waves would rise from the baked surface and distort the vision, and if the wind came up it would swirl fine dust particles into the heated air, making it even more difficult to see any distance.

He watched, and he could no longer keep still.

"Someone's coming, Joe."

The little man had been lying on his side, his back to the climbing sun, his bad hand extended before him. He sat up, surprise wiping the pain from his dark eyes.

"Coming?" He stood up. "Where?"

Vance Clark pointed to the growing dot. Joe Spain stared at it for a long moment. He had spent most of his working life on the Rocking Chair, and he had ridden across this lake as often as any man alive.

He said slowly, "Looks like it, anyhow."

"You mean it isn't?" Vance Clark turned to stare at him in dismay.

Joe Spain shrugged. "I've seen funny things in this country, Vance. I've seen waving trees and green leaves, and running springs, and mountain sheep. Who knows —"

"Mirages, yes."

"Who knows?"

Vance Clark looked again at the speck. He said suddenly, "There's more than one."

Joe Spain sat down. "Probably Petry decided we were too tough for the sun to kill and he's coming back to finish the job by hand."

Vance Clark kept on watching intently. He lost all idea of time. He was no longer conscious of the sun, growing hotter as the day wore toward noon. A quarter of an hour dragged by. A half. He said, "It's a rider with two led horses."

He stood up. Heat waves by now rose in a shimmering wall, so that the air seemed alive, and thick. A sharp fear that the rider would not see them sent him into a flurry of motions. He waved. He pulled the shirt from his back. He wanted to yell out, and then he realized that if he could see the rider clearly enough to tell that it was a woman, the woman must certainly see them.

Virginia Munger, he thought, Ginny.

He doubted his senses, yet he had to acknowledge what seemed to be a fact. He recognized Virginia although she was still better than half a mile distant.

He wiped his already cracked lips with the back of his hand and watched her come toward them, leading two saddled horses behind her. He did not wave, he did not speak. He had a sensation of unreality, as if this was not happening, as if it were a portion of a dream. But the girl was real enough, and so were the horses and so was the canteen hanging at her saddle.

He let Joe Spain drink first. The water was warm, and it had the slight sulphur taste peculiar to the country, but against his bruised lips it felt cool and invigorating.

After he had drunk sparingly he said, "I'm glad to see you, Kitten. Very, very glad."

She had swung down as soon as she had reached them, handing him the water bottle and waiting silently while they slaked their thirst. Now she stood staring at Joe Spain's hand, dark horror in her blue eyes.

"Who did that?" she asked in a husky whisper.

Neither answered, but she read the answer in their silence.

"Not Petry?"

46

Still they did not answer, and her voice was deep throated as she spoke with difficulty. "Vance, when is this going to end?"

"It would have ended for us today if you hadn't showed up," he said soberly. "We'd never have walked out of here alive."

"I couldn't believe it," she told him tensely. "Ernie Sylvester and two of the hands rode into town at midnight. I was sitting on the hotel porch. It was too hot to sleep. I heard them talking, laughing among themselves about the way Petry was putting you afoot on the lake. I went down to the livery as soon as I could and got the horses. I didn't make too good time, leading them and I was so afraid that I'd miss you."

He said, "You didn't. Let's get out of this oven." He wished he didn't have to talk to her about it. As children they had been very close, and as they grew older his feeling for her had altered and increased. He knew her so thoroughly, knew how her father's attempt to murder them must be eating into her sensitive spirit.

Joe Spain was trying to mount without the aid of his injured arm, and finding it hard. Vance walked over and helped the little rider into the saddle.

They rode in single file, the girl leading, Spain in the middle and Vance Clark bringing up the rear. The heat increased with the afternoon and the sun reflected from the hard-beaten sand scorched their skins. The air was so dry and hot that it seemed to sear their lungs.

It was a ride that Vance Clark knew he would never forget, never if he lived to be a thousand, and with each slow step their faltering horses took his anger swelled.

He wondered for a while if they would ever make it off the lake. The horses showed increasing signs of strain, and Joe Spain wilted in the saddle, clinging desperately with his good hand, his eyes at times closed, his small body weaving as if he were drunk.

The girl stood the ride better than either of them. She rode steadily, easily, and when the afternoon wind came up, swirling the fine dust over them in tiny sweeping clouds, she lifted her neckerchief to cover her mouth and nostrils and rode forward into the blast.

At four, the level surface of the lake gave way to the rising benchland, and they climbed a little. Vance Clark had realized almost from the first where she was heading — not for town, but for Brack Rick Spring, where a small trickle of water came out of the volcanic formation to make a tiny pool below the broken edge of the lava cap.

They reached this just before five. Vance Clark helped Joe Spain from the saddle and seated him in the shade of the rising rocks, and then he led the horses down for their first careful drink.

Afterward he squatted in the rock shade and smoked his first cigarette of the day, staring wordlessly back across the flat waste from which they had come.

The sun was still high in the western sky, but the wind had died and the dust gave way to a writhing shimmer of heat waves which came up into the cooling air from the overheated earth.

His lips were cracked and his fist-mauled face felt masklike, baked in some unyielding enamel.

Ginnie Munger came over to stand at his side. "What are you going to do, Vance?"

He didn't know. He heard the fear beneath her words, and he had nothing to tell her.

She said slowly, "I saved your life today."

He looked up at her quickly then, and his mouth tightened and his eyes narrowed. She said hastily,

"You're afraid I'm going to ask you not to fight back. Well, I'm not. I hate fighting, but I have to remember that if it hadn't been for my father your life wouldn't have been in danger. We'll call it even." She turned away and walked directly to her horse, her back straight and very rigid. She untied the animal and swung up, never once looking back. Vance Clark watched her, not attempting to hide the misery in his eyes, almost hoping that she would see it.

But she did not turn. He watched her until the trail wound its way about a rock shoulder and she was lost to sight.

Behind him, Joe Spain cleared his throat.

"There goes a woman," Joe said. "It's a damn shame her name is Munger."

CHAPTER
SIX

The lights of Elkhead were visible a long time before Vance Clark reached them. The trail twisted along the line of the swelling hills, skirting the dry surface of the lake and then cutting back across the sand to come into town from the east.

He met no one. This trail knew very little travel at any time and almost none during the hot summer months. He rode slowly, with Joe Spain at his side, leaning across to hold the smaller man in his saddle.

Spain's eyes were glazed and his face flushed under the new sunburn, and several times Vance Clark wondered if he would ever make it. But finally they came through the maze of dirt tracks lined by Mexican shacks into Boulder Street and rode down its wide length to the rear door of the livery.

The hostler was asleep inside. He roused as Vance rode into the runway and came out of the office, rubbing the sleep from his red-rimmed eyes. Vance helped Joe Spain down and the hostler caught sight of Spain's shattered hand. He gasped and awoke fully, the shocked expression on his dirty face suggesting that he knew what had happened yet could not believe it.

Vance said, "Watch him," and moved back into the livery office. He pulled out the drawer of the desk and lifted the battered forty-one which Pop Burrows always kept there. Then he took down the shotgun from the wall above the desk and shoved a shell into each of its barrels.

And after that he returned to the runway, carrying the weapons.

The hostler stared at the guns. Vance Clark said tightly, "If you know what's good for you, you never saw me ride in."

The hostler looked more uncertain than ever.

"Doc Clement in town?"

"I saw him going home an hour ago," the man said.

Without further word Vance slipped his free hand under Joe's arm and half led, half carried the little rider back to the rear street and along it to the square adobe hut which the doctor called home.

There was no light within the mean building and Vance frowned. It was unlike Clement to seek his bed this early, unless . . . He pushed across the dried yard and kicked on the door. No answer. He stood Joe against the dark wall, lifted the heavy iron latch and stepped into the small room.

Inside, the hot close air was heavy with the reek of whiskey. He struck a match and by its feeble flame saw the long thin form of Doc Clement, fully dressed, stretched face down on the sagging bed.

He swore then, but without much force. Clement being drunk did not really surprise him, and his weariness came over him in waves. The match burned his fingers and he dropped it. Fumbling for another, he struck it, found the lamp and lifted the smoked chimney. In the rising light he went back outside and brought Joe Spain in, saying in a soothing voice, "It will be all right in a little while, Joe."

A few inches of brownish liquid remained in the doctor's bottle. Clark poured a stiff drink and held it to Spain's lips and watched the little wave of life climb into the lined face.

Then he turned his attention to the snoring man on the bed. He hoisted him bodily to his feet, ignoring the muffled curses and protests which the action brought, and walked him to the yard. There he held Clement's head in the water barrel until it seemed that his victim would drown.

Doc Clement came to with a start. He wrestled, trying to free himself from the iron grip of the hands which held him, turning, spurting, finally recognizing his tormentor in the rectangle of light which flooded through the open door.

"Damn you, Vance, let me alone."

For answer Vance Clark ducked him again, releasing his grip and letting Clement push himself, dripping, away from the barrel.

"I'll kill you." At best Clement was a man of uncertain temper. At worst he could be as dangerous as a cornered rattler. But his ability to sober under stress was something Vance Clark had witnessed with amazement in the past.

"You all right, Doc?"

"How could I be all right when you've damn near drowned me, you idiot?"

"You sober?"

"Enough to kill you if I had a gun."

"It's Joe Spain," Vance said. "He's got a broken hand."

"Let it rot off."

"Come on, I'll get you some coffee." He led the reluctant doctor inside. Clement squinted around with red-veined eyes. His thin, hawk-like face showed the result of years of dissipation, but suddenly he was cold sober and businesslike, although his hands shook as he stripped off his wet shirt.

"What have we got here?"

Clark just grunted. He was busy building a fire in the stove and putting the blackened coffee pot on to boil.

Clement picked up a flour sack which apparently served him as a towel and scrubbed at his grizzled head.

"Better get him over on the bed," he said.

Vance Clark picked up Spain and laid him on the bed.

Clement walked over and examined the swollen hand and forearm. "You'll have to cut the shirt off him. There are scissors on the table."

Clark found the scissors and cut the sweat soaked shirt from Spain.

"Now get me some hot water. Better boil it." The doctor turned to the stove, tested the coffee pot, then poured himself a cup of the steaming liquid. It seemed impossible that he had been in a drunken stupor less than half an hour ago.

"What happened?"

Clark said, "The less you know, Doc, the less trouble you are apt to be getting into."

Clement said, "There's been talk around town for most of the afternoon. Some said the Double M put you boys afoot out on the dry lake." He appraised Vance Clark's burned face as he spoke. "From the looks of you I wouldn't be too surprised if the talk was true."

"The less you know, Doc, the better."

"It's a damn shame," Clement said. "This country is bad enough without a range war. Petry Munger must have lost what little sense he had to start with, and that wasn't much."

Vance ignored this. "What about Joe's hand?"

The doctor sat on the edge of the bed and picked up the swollen hand gingerly. Joe Spain groaned. He was only half conscious, but his face twisted with the pain of movement.

"Looks like they did a thorough job."

"Can you fix it?"

"I can set the bones. It should have been taken care of last night."

Clark regarded the doctor with cloudy eyes. "We weren't in any position to hunt a doctor last night."

Clement stared at him. "I'll bet you weren't. I'd like to know how you managed to make it off the lake at all in this kind of weather. I'd as soon try to walk through a blast furnace."

"A lot of people are going to try to figure that out," Clark said. "If anyone bothers to ask, you just tell them that maybe we're a little too tough to die. Let's get to work on Joe."

Clement got to work. He was a better doctor drunk than most were sober, but by the time he finished splinting and wrapping that mangled hand he was sweating profusely.

Joe was out, a combination of pain and whiskey and laudanum. He lay small and curiously shrunken on the sagging bed, the harsh lines of his face softened and eased by unconsciousness.

Vance Clark spread his hands helplessly. "I don't know what to do with him. If Petry Munger finds him in that shape there's no telling what he'll do."

The doctor flushed. "Petry Munger or no one else is going to touch a patient of mine while he's in my house."

"Not while you're sober," Vance agreed cruelly.

Clement drew himself up, his thin body standing straight and tall. "You don't think I can let the bottle alone?"

"No."

"Damn it, I will." Clement's mouth worked. "I'll not have a drink as long as Joe is in this house."

Clark wanted to believe that. He had always liked Clement, feeling a little sorry for him as a strong man sometimes feels sorry for a weaker one. "You're all right, Doc." He picked up the shotgun and started for the door.

Clement said, "Don't be a damn fool, Vance. There's half a dozen Double M riders in town right now."

"There would have to be twenty to stop me," Clark said savagely. "This country has to learn not to bury the Rocking Chair before it's dead."

He went out, closing the door behind him. The doctor stood staring at the panel. Then he turned slowly and glanced at the whiskey bottle which still held one full drink.

The tip of his parched tongue came out to run around his dry lips. He sighed. He picked up the bottle, crossed to the door, opened it and heaved the bottle into the yard. It broke with a small popping noise, but Vance Clark was too far up the street to hear.

He passed the darkened hotel porch wearily and came on to stop and peer across the top of the batwing doors of the Palace at the smoky room beyond.

Two poker games were going at the rear, and four men stood against the bar, but the people he sought were at a table in the middle of the room.

There were four of them. His mouth thinned as he recognized Ernie Sylvester and Ray Pinker. The two other men he had not seen before.

He guessed that these must be some of the new hands Petry Munger was importing. He steadied himself against the exhaustion which rose through him like an eddying wave. Then using the twin barrels of the shotgun to knock the doors apart, he stepped into the room.

Ernie Sylvester thrust back his chair and came to his feet in one violent convulsion.

Ray Pinker came up also, looking scared and uncertain. He stood beyond the table, holding his hands away from his sides in a gesture which said plainly that he wanted no part of a fight.

The two new men twisted to see what had caused the sudden motion. They sat frozen in their seats, their heads turned, their eyes on the gun in Vance's hands.

The card game had ceased. The men at the bar and the two bartenders clung to their places as if all action had been squeezed out of the room.

Clark came forward until only ten feet separated him from the men at the table. He stopped.

"Ernie, come here."

The words served as a trigger to release sound within the room. Someone let out a long-held breath. The men at the bar began to shift their positions. Sylvester's face turned a deeper red.

"Go to hell," he said.

"Come here," Vance Clark said.

"Put that damn scattergun down and I'll take you, any time, Clark."

Vance Clark's voice was very cold. "This isn't a contest, Ernie. This is for keeps. What chance did you give us when you put us afoot on the lake?"

"I'd like to know how in hell you got off. When I find out who helped you —"

"Come here."

Sylvester did not move. Vance Clark stalked forward, eyes watchful, circling the table, never shifting the angle of the gun which covered the seated men.

As he came into reaching distance Sylvester grabbed at the gun barrels with both hands. It was what Clark had been waiting for. He did not pull the triggers. Instead he swung the heavy barrels in an arc and crashed them against the side of Sylvester's head, as heavily, as brutally as he could.

The man went down. He fell all at once, as if his body had suddenly become unjointed. It happened so rapidly that no one in the big room was prepared for it, and even as he struck, Vance Clark jumped backward, his shotgun again covering the room.

Ray Pinker said in a strangled voice, "You killed him."

"His head's too hard," Vance Clark said. "You want part of it, Ray?"

Pinker answered by spreading his hands wide, away from his belted guns. The other two Double M riders sat still at the table.

Vance Clark said, "A word of advice, Ray. Ernie filed on the valley above Stinking Water. Tell him to get out. A man won't be safe in that cabin. I won't warn him again."

Pinker wet his lips. "A man's got a right to file on land." He sounded scared but stubborn.

"If he does it honestly." Clark's voice was like a cutting knife. "If he means to prove up on it, and live on it. But you know and I know that a man couldn't make a living on a section of land in this country. Ernie filed on that piece merely to block the Rocking Chair away from water, so that we can't use the grass on that whole side of North Mountain. Well, it won't work. Put up fences and I'll cut them. And whoever tries to live in that cabin will be shot."

He stared hard at the two men still seated at the table. "As for you, you're new here. I'm telling you to get out while you can. Your crew tried to kill me last night. I'm a hard man to kill. Just remember that."

He backed toward the door. Once through it he raced across to the shadows of the opposite building, seeking shelter in their gloom.

He had hardly reached it when the Palace door burst open. Calmly he raised the shotgun and fired the left barrel. They jumped back inside. Laughing silently he sprinted down the street for the livery. He was riding out before they broke from the saloon a second time.

CHAPTER
SEVEN

The Rocking Chair yard was dark and deserted. He crossed the baked ground and stepped down beside the corral gate, pulling the saddle and bridle from the weary horse.

He let the animal into the enclosure and turned, intending to head for the bunkhouse. But then he saw a light come on in the main house and heard Grover call from the porch.

He had no desire to talk to anyone that night, certainly not the ranch owner, but he realized that this was something he could not avoid. He reached the steps and saw Gilbert Grover standing in the light from the hall. The smaller figure of Judy appeared beside Grover, and Vance heard her say, "We were worried." He climbed the steps and managed a slow smile for her.

Grover's voice reached him, laden with worry. "Spain's not with you?"

"I left him at Doc Clements." He felt their questions and moved past them, suddenly conscious of his dirty clothes, of the sweat smell which came into the house with him.

They saw the marks on his face and the pain grayness about his lips, and Judy said quickly, "I'll get some coffee," and hurried back along the hall as he followed Grover into the room.

The mounted birds stared down at him with their glassy eyes and he wondered tiredly if his own eyes did not look as bad.

Grover had gone back to his table desk and seated himself behind it, saying in his quiet voice,

"You had some trouble, I judge?"

Vance Clark told him then. He spared no words, laying out the whole bleak picture for the ranch owner. "They've got us cut off from Stinking Water. They've got the grass and come winter they'll push their cows across from South Mountain and feed them on the bench. But next spring they won't shove them back again. They'll hold them here and gradually push us off the range."

As he talked he was conscious that Judy had come from the kitchen and stood just inside the door, listening. He did not turn. He knew her well enough to guess the quick anger his words had kindled in her.

Gilbert Grover's reaction surprised him however. In all the years he had known the ranch owner he had never seen Grover exhibit true anger. But as he told about the breaking of Joe Spain's hand, and of their being taken out onto the lake to die, he saw Grover's fine eyes darken and the sharp red come into his cheeks.

Grover said tightly, "How much can you misjudge a man? I took Petry Munger and made him what he was."

This, Vance Clark felt, was not exactly true. Petry Munger was just what he had always been, a pirate who rode a horse instead of a fighting ship, a ruthless man who had started with nothing and had fought his way to the top by stepping on lesser men.

It was true that the name and credit of the Rocking Chair had been behind him during his climb, but even without this Munger would have made something of himself. It was built into the tough fiber of the man.

"The question now," Vance Clark said, "is what we mean to do. If we leave them at Stinking Water we might as well throw away our branding irons and quit."

Grover stared through the cases of mounted birds, unseeing. Judy came forward carrying a tray with three steaming cups of coffee. Her dark eyes met Vance Clark's across the tray. He saw trouble there, and anger, and something else which he could not quite fathom.

She said, "What do you mean to do?"

"I've already warned Ernie Sylvester to get off that claim. I'm going to get some men somewhere and haze about a thousand head of cattle down onto that hay. If we can't have it at least our beef might as well eat it while there's some left."

"If you do that you'll have a bunch of U.S. marshals down on our necks," Grover said. "There must be some other way."

"There isn't." Vance Clark swallowed his coffee at a single gulp and marched from the house. He heard Grover call after him but he did not stop. He was too tired for useless argument this night.

The bunkhouse was chill and empty. He undressed without bothering to light a lamp, and wrapped himself in his blankets, missing Joe Spain, feeling alone, feeling helpless. It was a mood which he did not well understand. For most of his life he had sensed the power of the ranch around him. It had been like a father, a protector, spreading its shield over all its employees, and now that shield was gone.

He went to sleep but roused with the same bitter thought. The bunkhouse was still. The ranch yard was quiet. He lay there feeling the ache of his stiffened muscles, the soreness of his bruised face. If he had needed anything to remind him of the trouble they were in, these two things did.

He rolled over and saw that the bunkhouse door was open and that Judy Grover stood in the entrance watching him. He knew then what had roused him, and came up onto one elbow.

She said, "I hated to wake you, but I'm worried."

"Worried?"

"Father rode out before I was up. I didn't realize he was gone until I went into his office half an hour ago and found this note."

Vance Clark sat up, pulling the blankets around him, holding out one hand for the note.

She came across the rough boards to pass it to him. He stared at the ink scrawl, his brain still slow from sleep fog.

"Am going to see Petry," the note read. "This trouble has gone far enough."

He swore softly under his breath. "Where'd he go, town?"

"I suppose so."

"Get me some coffee while I dress."

She nodded and left the bunkhouse.

Thirty minutes later when he stepped from the kitchen he found that she had saddled not only his horse but her own bay. He thought about it for a moment, then lifted himself into his saddle. He knew her too well to argue. If she had made up her mind to go with him she would go, and nothing that he could say would stop her.

They rode in silence, grimly, each wrapped in bitter thoughts. In a few short weeks their whole lives had changed. Once a trip to town had been an occasion for gaiety, but there was no gaiety here, no sense of lift as they breasted the shoulder of North Mountain and dropped down toward the edge of the sink where Elkhead lay, its frame buildings weathered and bleached to pewter by the desert sun, hard to distinguish from their adobe neighbors.

They came into the long street, quiet and deserted in the noon hush. They pulled up before the hotel rail, stepping down and climbing the creaking steps and welcoming the half darkness of the long, narrow hotel lobby.

No one was behind the high desk, but the smell of food and the clatter of dishes came from the dining room at the rear.

Judy Grover turned toward it automatically but Clark stopped her with a gesture. "We don't want to talk in front of a room full of people." He used the hand bell and they stood before the desk, waiting until the hotel man appeared.

Justin Press was small, with a big nose and very little hair on the top of his round head. He was noted for his whining voice and his fear of his large, overstuffed wife. He hurried out, wiping his hands on the white apron he always wore while serving in the dining room, and when he recognized them his thin mouth pulled down at the corners.

"Look, Vance, you know what time it is, and you know I've got twenty hungry wolves in there yammering for their vittles. What's the idea of ringing the bell?"

"Gil Grover rode in this morning," Clark said quickly. "Who did he see and where is he now?"

Something like malicious mirth came up into the hotel man's pale eyes. "You Rocking Chair people are singing pretty small these days, ain't you?"

Vance Clark realized suddenly that the hotel man hated him. The knowledge came as something of a shock. He had taken Press more or less for granted, but he sensed now that Press had always been envious of the big ranch and of the people who lived upon it.

He said calmly, "How we sing, high or low, is no affair of yours. Answer my question, Justin."

Press stared back at him. Obviously he would have loved to refuse and to make his refusal as insulting as possible. But Vance Clark's eyes checked the impulse.

"Gil come in here for breakfast," Press said grudgingly. "He was some worked up. I've never seen him so worked up. He waited until Austin come in for breakfast, and then they left together."

Vance Clark made no effort to hide his surprise. "Gil Grover left here with Bryce Austin?"

"That's what I said, and an hour later I saw him ride out of town by the south road." He grinned at them sourly. "And I don't care if he never comes back. We can do without Rocking Chair trade from now on."

He turned and flounced back into the dining room, slamming the connecting door behind him. Vance glanced at Judy. Her cheeks were red, her dark eyes smoky, and her small fists clenched.

"The sniveling rat." She said it through tight set teeth. "As long as I can remember he crawled around when either Father or Petry were in the room."

"And he hated all of us then." Vance Clark looked at the closed door.

"Why should he hate us?" The girl's words were almost a cry. "We never did anything to him."

"Or for him." Vance Clark added this under his breath. "I never realized before how most of the people in this country must have felt about the ranch. We were the only really big outfit in this part of the state, and Petry Munger never let anyone forget it."

She was turning slowly toward the street. "They should hate Petry, not us."

"It's the ranch they hate, the name, Rocking Chair. They won't stop to figure out that it was Petry who gave them trouble. In the showdown they'll stand with Petry because he turned against the ranch."

He could tell by her expression that she did not believe him, but he changed the subject. "Let's have a talk with Bryce Austin."

She followed him from the hotel in silence, keeping abreast as they moved down the street to the foot of the steep stairs which led upward to the office rooms above Hall's Hardware. Here she stopped.

"You go up and talk to him," she said. "If I go I'll say something that I'll probably regret."

He nodded.

"I'll go out to Doc Clement's and see how Joe Spain is." She did not wait for his answer but headed down the street. For a moment he remained motionless, watching after her. Then he climbed the stairs and thrust open the unmarked door to the lawyer's office.

Bryce Austin was in his shirt sleeves, seated before his roll-top desk. His face bore the marks of their fight, and his dark eyes glowed a little, like a cat's in the darkness.

He did not speak. He sat unmoving. His eyes strayed toward the gunbelt which hung from a hook in the far wall, then came back to the man who had paused just inside the office door.

"What do you want?" he said.

Clark took his time closing the door, making it a kind of ceremony, as if he were shutting them away from the outside world. Then he walked to the desk and stood over the seated man.

"I don't like you," he said. "Since you came into this country there's been nothing but trouble."

Bryce Austin managed to smile, although his twisting lips showed no sign of real amusement. "So?"

"I just thought I'd tell you." Clark paused. "Gilbert Grover came in this morning. He met you at the hotel and then came on down here with you. What did he want?"

Austin laughed outright. "Why not ask him? You're his foreman. Or doesn't he trust you any farther than I do?"

"I'm asking you."

"And if I don't tell you?"

Vance Clark's right hand snaked out with startling suddenness. He caught Bryce Austin by the front of his shirt and lifted the man clear of the chair, jerking him foreward until their faces were only inches apart.

"I licked you the other night," he said quietly. "I'm just waiting for an excuse to do it again. I don't like being left afoot on the dry lake."

He shoved Austin from him, so that the backs of Austin's knees struck the edge of the chair seat. He collapsed into it, his face white with hard-held anger, his eyes so dark that they were almost coal black.

"If you ever lay hands on me again —"

"What did Gilbert Grover want?"

Bryce Austin wiped his mouth with the back of his hand, obviously fighting for control. When he spoke it was in a lower tone, a tight tone, as if he were determined to keep his temper.

"He wanted to sell the Rocking Chair. He said that he wasn't a fighter, that he wanted no part of a range war. He wanted me to talk to Petry."

"You're a liar."

Austin said slowly, "You drive a man hard, Clark."

"Not half as hard as I mean to drive you."

The man at the desk wiped his mouth again. "That's what Gilbert told me. Gilbert said he realized we had you licked, since we've filed on the hay fields and the canyon above Stinking Water, but you wouldn't quit. He's afraid of what you'll do. He doesn't want federal marshals in here, and he doesn't want a lot of people dead."

Despite himself Vance Clark was haunted by the feeling that the lawyer might be telling the truth. Gilbert Grover was not a fighter. He had no use for violence.

"What did you tell him?"

"That he'd have to talk to Petry. That since the court case at the capital the thing was out of my hands."

"Where's Petry?"

"At Stinking Water. The last I saw of Gilbert he was headed in that direction."

CHAPTER
EIGHT

Lem Stewart was just coming from the sheriff's office as Vance Clark passed and he called sharply, "A minute, Vance."

Vance Clark stopped. He watched the sheriff's bent figure move stiffly down the three steps and cross the boardwalk toward him.

For as long as he could remember Stewart had been the sheriff of this county, a slow-moving, easygoing man who had spent most of his days in one of the chairs on the hotel porch, his work limited mostly to serving a few papers for the county judge and collecting taxes.

The jail behind the office seldom held anyone more vicious than a rider drunk from a Saturday night dance who had let off excess spirit by shooting into the air above the main street.

Vance waited, studying the sheriff's lined face, guessing how unhappy and ill at ease the man was. Stewart stopped before him, removed his hat and wiped the beaded sweat from his almost bald head.

"Hear you had a little trouble the other day."

Vance said nothing. It had never occurred to him to report to Stewart the fact that he and Joe Spain had been put afoot on the dry lake. He would sooner throw the old man into a cave full of rattlesnakes than send him against Ernie Sylvester and the Double M riders.

The sheriff looked up at him, his faded blue eyes troubled. He sighed. "I'm some older than you, Vance. I'll be seventy-one come next grass, I've seen my share of trouble."

Vance still held himself silent, and the old man's voice sharpened. "It's been a long time since there was much sheriffing to do around here. Petry Munger kind of policed the country when he was running Rocking Chair, but now that he and Gilbert have split I won't stand for any rough stuff."

"Tell Petry that," Clark said.

"I have told him, and he knows I mean it."

"Have you seen Joe Spain's hand?"

"Yes, and I saw what you did to Ernie Sylvester. I tell you I won't stand for it. I told Gilbert so this morning."

For the first time Vance looked at the older man with real interest. "You did? Where?"

"Just about where you're standing. He'd been over to see how Joe was making out and I could tell by the way he walked that he was mad. It ain't often Gilbert lets his temper get away from him, but he was riled up this morning. First time he ever reminded me of his daddy."

He stopped as if expecting Vance to speak, but Clark held his comment and the old man went on. "He wanted me to go out and run Petry's men off the hay fields. I told him I had no legal right to do it and he didn't either. He turned away and went to his horse and rode off."

"Toward Stinking Water?"

The old man nodded. "I haven't been easy since he left. I'll ride out with you if you like. He was packing a gun, and it's years since I saw Gil Grover pack a gun."

"Thanks, but I won't need you."

A stubborn look came into Lem Stewart's faded eyes. "I'll just ride along anyway." He turned and headed for the livery stable.

Vance Clark stared after him. Then he saw Judy come from Doc Clement's yard and moved up the sidewalk to meet her.

"How's Joe?"

"Like a bear whose winter nap's been spoiled. He's sitting there planning what he'll do to Petry Munger when his hand heals."

"What did Doc say about the hand?"

"That it will never be right again, likely stiff, and he's not certain Joe can use the fingers. What did you learn from Austin?"

"He says your father is trying to sell the ranch."

Her eyes darkened until they were nearly black. "He's lying. Father would never sell the ranch. He figures it's mine. He's certainly not trying to sell without consulting me."

"Would you sell?"

"Of course not."

"Even if it meant losing everything?"

The muscles tightened along her delicate jawline. "There were Grovers on the Rocking Chair before Petry Munger was even a saddle bum, and there will be a Grover on this ranch when the last Munger is dead. Let's find Gil."

He said, "Lem Stewart is riding with us."

"We don't need him."

"I don't think we have much to say," Vance said mildly. "After all, he is the sheriff. Here he comes now."

They rode out of town in silence, conscious that a number of people watched them from the sidewalks and from the half shadow of the store doorways, and Vance Clark's mouth twisted as the thought came that these watchers were probably betting on their chance of survival once they came up with Petry Munger.

His hand strayed to the worn gun at his belt. It had been a present from Virginia Munger on his sixteenth birthday, and certainly neither of them had dreamed at the time that he would ever be called upon to use it against her father.

He had been proud of it then, and of the belt and holster that went with it, but now the grip was scarred from contact with the brush.

Riding at his side, Lem Stewart saw the gesture. The old man had worn a star for nearly fifty years, as marshal, deputy and finally sheriff, and his lips, no longer full red but a little blue with age, pressed together as he studied the younger man.

Ahead, Judy Grover set a pace which forced them to press their horses to keep up with her. She rode as she usually did, as though she were driven, for there was nothing temperate about this small girl.

The trail led around the jutting curve of North Mountain, passing Black Springs and climbing over a fragment of weathered lava cap to run along the high shoulder of the bench, a good five hundred feet above the hard-packed sand of the dry lake below.

From far off they had a glimpse of the green checkerboard which was the hay fields, and as they drew closer they saw a crew at work below the camp. Judy's shoulders stiffened and she came erect in the saddle. She increased her pace as the trail crossed a hogback and dropped downward to the line camp.

Petry Munger and two hands were in the yard when they rode up, and the owner of the Double M made no effort to hide his surprise at sight of the sheriff. He said mockingly as Lem Stewart reined in and eased his old body forward in the saddle, "You're a long way from town, sheriff. I disremember when I've seen you so far from a chair on the hotel porch."

Stewart grunted.

Petry pointedly ignored Vance Clark, but his voice was courtesy itself when he said to the girl, "Nice of you to ride out and watch us hay, Judy."

"Where's Dad?" she snapped.

"Why, he was here a couple of hours back. Rode up to see how Ernie's new cabin was getting along." Petry chuckled. "Wouldn't hardly believe that Ernie had fenced the canyon above the springs."

Without warning Judy drove her spurs into the startled bay. The horse leaped forward. She wrenched at the bit and it reared, its front legs pawing the air.

Petry Munger tried to spring backward. His heel caught and he went down, and Judy Grover rode over him.

It was more the bay's instinct than the girl's intent that kept the hoofs from striking the fallen man.

Lem Stewart let out a protesting yell. One of the Double M hands stood with his mouth open, paralyzed by surprise. The bay spooked across the yard and Judy fought it, trying to bring the horse around.

Vance Clark sensed that she meant to turn and ride back over Petry Munger before the man could struggle to his feet, and he reacted automatically. He jumped his own horse into motion, driving across to head off the angry girl, catching the bridle rein as the bay came around and jerking it to a quivering halt.

They sat thus, side by side, their knees touching, their eyes locked. Judy's hand came up and Vance braced himself for a blow. Then she controlled herself with visible effort. She yanked the line free of his hand, kicked her spurs into the horse's flank and went out of the yard at a dead run.

He sat staring after her, too startled to move, until sound behind him made him twist in the saddle in time to see Petry Munger come slowly up from the ground.

For once, Petry Munger was shaken. He stood gaping after the girl as she drove her horse along the sloping trail which followed the ditch toward the springs above.

Then Munger turned without a word and moved into the house. The sheriff's old eyes met those of Vance and there was a gleam in their faded depths. But he only said as he pushed his horse forward, "Maybe we'd better go after her."

Vance Clark nodded and they rode out of the yard together, the old man making noises under his breath which might have been chuckles.

"She reminded me of her grandfather for a minute," he said. "I'll bet Petry won't forget this day in a hurry."

As they climbed the looping trail Vance looked back across the hay fields. Petry Munger might have been knocked down, but his haying crews were busy cutting the grass that would mean failure or existence to the Rocking Chair during the coming winter. It would take more than riding over Munger with a horse to win for them now.

They caught Judy easily enough. She had halted her horse above the springs and sat staring down at the water backed up behind the earth dam. She offered no apology. She just urged her animal forward and they circled around the manmade pond and started to climb the canyon toward the top of North Mountain.

Beyond a curve they came against a line of fencing stretching from one steep canyon wall to the other, completely blocking their path.

They pulled up before the wire which in its newness glistened under the sun's rays, and as they sat there the sharp, whip-like crack of a rifle sounded from the area above them.

For seconds nobody moved. Then Judy Grover put her horse at the fence, clearing it with a swallow-like leap.

Vance Clark shouted after her to wait. The animal he rode was not a jumper and he knew it would never go over the top strand of wire. With an oath he swung down. He had no tools, and as far as he could see there was no gate. Whoever had put up the fence had intended it for a barrier, but the posts were new set, shallow set, the earth around them only indifferently tamped, and the wire loosely strung. He seized the center strand with both hands, shaking the post back and forth, working it loose from its bedded hole.

He heard a second rifle shot and then a third, and afterward the flatter sound of a forty-five.

The post came loose with a suddenness which almost caused Vance to fall backward. He threw it down but Lem Stewart rode forward before Vance could get back into his saddle.

He caught the sheriff before the old man reached the bend in the canyon, and they came around the jutting promontory together. The shooting had stopped, and they hauled up when they saw the outline of the cabin.

The building had not been completed. Its log walls were up, and the line of its roof rafters, but it still lacked a door and window frames.

As they pulled up a shot came from within the cabin, and they discovered Judy Grover behind some rocks to the left, her gun in her hand, her horse straying off across the small stream.

Someone within the cabin fired at Judy and she returned the shots with a quick burst from her hand gun. Vance Clark slid out of his saddle, jerking the rifle from the boot and landing at a run, zigzagging to reach the girl.

A bullet from the cabin whistled over his head. He dropped to his knees, crawling the last dozen feet until he reached Judy. She was crouched down, reloading her gun, and she gave him a tight, angry grin as he came up.

"Who's in the cabin?"

"Ernie Sylvester, I think. It looked like him. He and Ray Pinker were over to the left, shooting up at those rocks." She indicated a place on the canyon wall to the right and above the house. "I think Dad's up there."

Vance Clark glanced toward the rocks but could see nothing. "What happened to Pinker?"

"When I started to shoot Ernie ran for the cabin. Pinker made it up the rocks." She had her gun reloaded and stood up deliberately, throwing two shots at the doorless opening in the log wall, drawing shots in return.

Vance Clark pulled her down savagely. "You fool. You'll get yourself killed."

She glared at him. "They've done something to Dad. I know it. If he isn't dead why isn't he shooting?"

Vance Clark had been thinking the same thing, but he tried to keep the fear out of his voice.

"We don't even know your father came this way."

"He did. I saw his horse above the cabin when I first got here."

He stared at her. The shooting from the cabin had stopped again and they heard Lem Stewart shout up the canyon. "Whoever you are in there, come out. This is Stewart."

There was a soundless wait. Then Ernie Sylvester called, "Tell them to hold their fire, Sheriff."

78

Stewart rode up, looking curiously shrunken on the back of his big horse. "You heard him, Judy, Vance." He put himself between the pile of rocks and the cabin as if he did not trust either Judy or Clark. "All right," he said. "Come out."

Ernie Sylvester stepped into view. He carried his rifle in the crook of his arm, raising the other hand in a gesture of half surrender.

"All right, Sheriff." He dropped the rifle to the ground and walked toward the mounted man.

CHAPTER
NINE

"We didn't mean to shoot him," Sylvester said. "I was working on the cabin when he jumped his horse over the fence and rode in. Ray had been working on the fence at the upper end of the canyon."

They listened tensely. The sheriff still held his saddle. Vance Clark and Judy stood beside his horse, at the foot of the canyon wall, with Sylvester facing them.

"I was on the roof," Sylvester went on. "I didn't have a gun with me and he threw down on me before I could move. He told me to jump down and get my horse and ride out. I jumped. There wasn't much else I could do."

Judy made a noise deep in her throat. She turned and started for the canyon side, calling her father's name as she went. Vance Clark caught her shoulder. "Let me," he said, and passed her and began to climb the rocks.

There had been a slide here long ago, and soil had drifted down to fill the crevice and brush had found a slender footing in its shallow depth.

He had no difficulty in the climb. The face, while too steep for a horse, offered no problem for a man. He was halfway up before he found the blood, still smeary, upon a bare rock.

He paused, looking up, calling, "Gil, Gil, are you all right?"

There was no answer. He climbed on, and he found Gilbert Grover dead, crouched behind the shelter of the rocks, his rifle fallen beside him.

Vance Clark stood numbly on the rim of rocks, looking downward at the owner of the Rocking Chair. Then Judy's voice roused him.

"Vance, Vance, is Father all right?"

He knew no way to break the force of the shock, and made no attempt. "He's dead." He stepped over the rim and knelt beside the lifeless man, lifting his slight body, holding him thus while he searched for wounds. He found only one bullet hole in the body, directly in the center of Gilbert Grover's back.

Vance Clark never remembered his return down the slide. He moved automatically, with no conscious direction from his brain.

As he neared the bottom Ernie Sylvester took a step forward as if to help, and Clark lashed at him with sudden fury.

"Don't touch him!"

Sylvester jerked backward as if he had been slapped in the face. Vance lay his burden on the ground, and Judy dropped to her knees beside the slender body.

She did not cry. She simply knelt there, making no effort to touch her father.

Lem Stewart had seen death many times and in many forms, but he was visibly moved as he stepped from his horse and confronted Ernie Sylvester.

The redhead said sharply, as if in answer to the unspoken indictment, "I didn't shoot him. Ray Pinker did."

"In the back," Vance Clark said.

"He was going to shoot me." Ernie Sylvester's voice rose an octave. "He had the drop on me. He was going to shoot me."

Vance Clark's tone was even and expressionless. "You're lying, Ernie. There's no blood on the lower rocks. I don't know exactly what happened. I don't suppose we'll ever know, unless you talk, but I think Gil was trying to get away from the two of you, climbing the canyon wall, and one of you hit him in the back. He didn't die where he was hit. He had enough left to climb to those rocks before he died."

Ernie Sylvester half turned as if to walk to the house. Suddenly Judy was on her feet, pulling the gun from her holster.

Lem Stewart caught her, moving swiftly for one of his age, and he twisted the big gun from her small fingers. "Easy, Judy. Let the law take care of this."

She blazed at him. "When did the law ever settle anything in this country? Help me, Vance."

But Vance Clark was no longer paying attention to her. A distant shout from the lower end of the canyon had reached him. He had seen four Double M riders led by Petry Munger spurring through the gap in the lower fence.

Behind him he heard Ernie Sylvester's quick, relieved laugh. He heard the redhead say, "Now we'll see. Now we'll see," and had to resist the impulse to swing and empty his gun into the grinning face.

Petry Munger and his men swept forward and jerked their straining horses to a sliding stop.

"What goes on here?" Munger roared.

"Murder!" Judy wrenched herself loose from Lem Stewart's grasp. "You're as much to blame as if you had pulled the trigger, Petry!"

Munger sat heavily in the saddle, his gaze going beyond the girl to rest briefly on his former partner's still form. Then he spoke to Sylvester. "What happened?"

Sylvester repeated the story he had told, and Munger listened impassively. "Where's Ray Pinker?"

Sylvester shrugged. "When the girl rode up and started shooting at us I ran for the house, but Ray had his horse up by the north fence. I guess he made for it."

Munger glanced up-canyon. A bend in the sharp walls hid the upper fence. "Pinker shot Gil?"

Sylvester nodded.

Munger turned to the sheriff. "How many men do you need?"

Lem Stewart's quick surprise showed. "Men? For what?"

"For a posse." Munger was suddenly impatient. "I want Pinker brought in. I want him to stand trial."

Judy said furiously, "So your hand-picked jury can whitewash him."

Munger ignored her. "I don't want the country to think I'm backing murder, Lem. Gilbert Grover was trespassing on this land. If what Sylvester says is true, I want the facts known."

Vance Clark said, "So you'd not be trying Pinker. You'd be trying a dead man."

No one spoke. He took his time looking at them all and then he said to Judy, "I'll get your father's horse. We'll take him home."

No one interfered as he mounted his own animal and rode up the canyon to rope Gilbert Grover's straying mount. He rounded the curve and found the animal grazing against the partly completed fence.

Still no one spoke when he came back, nor was he offered help as he wrapped the body in a saddle blanket and lashed it across the horse. He had no other choice. There was no wagon, and the trail over which they must ride would not have accommodated one.

Left to himself he might have taken Gil Grover's body into the graveyard beside the little church in town, but he knew Judy's feelings without asking her. Grover's father was buried on the hillside above the ranch yard and Judy would want Gil to rest there also.

He finished the lashing. The old sheriff walked over to him, saying in a low tone, "I'll take care of Pinker, Clark."

Vance nodded and swung stiffly into the saddle. With Judy he rode up the winding canyon, past the postline of the new fence, and branched off on the narrow trail which followed the bulging contour of the mountain toward the home ranch.

It was well after midnight when they came into the deserted yard. Vance lifted the body from the horse and laid it on the porch. After unsaddling, he went to the small blacksmith shop for tools and lumber, and built the box.

That done, he found a pick and a spade and climbed the rise to the point where the single stone marked the resting place of the ranch's founder. He dug the hole. The soil was thin, underlaid with a slanting strata of bedrock which only powder would have penetrated.

He finished the shallow grave and returned for the box, half carrying it, half dragging it up the slope. Afterward he came back down for the body, since it would have been impossible for him to handle the combined weight alone.

There was no ceremony. He worked quietly, doggedly, nailing the lid down and refilling the grave. Not until he had thrown the last shovel full into place and turned away did he know that Judy had come up the rise and was watching him.

On impulse he stretched out his hand. She took it and he led her back down to the house as one might lead a small child. At the edge of the porch he paused and she said in a toneless voice, "Come in. I'll get something to eat."

"I'm not hungry."

"You've got to eat, Vance. You haven't had anything since morning."

He followed her down the length of long hall and into the big square kitchen. A fire was burning in the black range and a pot of coffee bubbled on the stove.

She poured him a cup and he sat down beside the square table, its board top whitened by years of scrubbing. He sat quietly by, watching as she sliced cold meat, and put butter and bread and jam upon the table.

This room had always seemed to him the very center of the ranch's life. He had lived at the bunkhouse, and taken most of his meals with the crew, but during the long winter evenings he had often been invited here. And here he had eaten with the two girls and Gil Grover, listening to the laughter and enjoying the heat from the big stove.

He had learned to dance here, Gil Grover strumming his guitar while the girls took turns teaching him. But the laughter was gone, and the pleasure, and the bustle which had once filled the big yard. They were alone, the two of them. They were all that remained of the Rocking Chair.

Suddenly he wanted to be out of the room. He had the feeling that the walls were pressing in on him, holding him, imprisoning him, but a look at Judy made him forget himself.

The shock of Gil Grover's death had been bad for him, but it had been much worse for Judy. She sat down and began mechanically to eat. He tried to guess her thoughts, but her small face was unreadable. She had always been thus, self-contained and competent even as a child.

He said slowly, "Do you want to talk about things now, or would you rather wait?"

She raised her dark eyes. "What's there to talk about?"

He thought about the wreck of the big ranch, of the fact that they had no crew, that Petry Munger had stolen their winter hay and was even now fencing them away from Stinking Water.

He said, "The future, I guess, the ranch, what you mean to do. You can't very well stay here alone."

"Why not?"

"Well —" suddenly he felt embarrassed, "people will talk, just you and me, alone on the ranch."

"Let them." Her tone showed her utter indifference to what anyone in the country thought or said. "We've got to get a crew, a fighting one. If Petry Munger thinks he's won his fight because Gil is dead he has another think coming."

Something in her voice made Vance Clark wince. Something about her attitude frightened him.

She showed no sign of grief, not even a sign of anger; only an iron determination. She was too young to feel this way. It seemed as if all emotion had been burned out of her, as if she had lost all semblance of human feeling.

He said, "Let's not talk about it now. Let's wait until morning."

She shook her head. "There's something to do first. I looked in Gil's desk when I came in. I found these." She pulled two envelopes out of her apron pocket. Vance Clark frowned questioningly, not understanding.

She said, "Apparently Gil expected trouble when he rode out this morning. He left two notes, one for you and one for me." She extended the one which bore his name and the loose flap told him that it had been opened.

Again she answered his unspoken question.

"I opened it," she said flatly.

He pulled out the folded sheet. He read:

Dear Vance:

I always wanted a son and never had one. I think that this more than anything else accounts for my feeling for you.

If you have occasion to read this it will be because I am dead, and I will be leaving you the legacy of a range war. Perhaps the trouble is largely my fault for turning over to Petry as much of the authority on the ranch as I did. But whatever the reason, the fact remains that we are all in deep trouble. I ask one last favor of you then. I have watched you and Judy grow up together. I have watched hopefully for signs of mutual affection. Unfortunately I have failed to observe any. But also I am sure that neither of you have romantic attachments which might make what I am going to suggest impossible. It is my last wish that you two marry, that you share the ranch together, and that you carry it on as best you can . . .

There was no signature, but there could be no doubt that the letter was in Gil Grover's hand. Vance Clark sat motionless, his mind whirling. He could not force himself to look at Judy, until he remembered that she had read the letter. If she had not wanted him to see it, she would have destroyed it.

He looked up to find her watching him, and his lips felt wooden as he asked, "Is that what you want, Judy?"

She nodded. There was no hint of color in her cheeks, no embarrassment.

"It will be the simplest way," she said.

CHAPTER
TEN

The news of Gilbert Grover's death shook Virginia Munger badly. As a child she had looked up to him, although she had never really liked him. For her he had been always a little withdrawn.

When she had first come to the ranch to live, her father had been the foreman and Grover the owner, and she had regarded the small man who spent so much time with his rock collection and his stuffed birds as something of an eccentric, to be avoided when possible. When their paths crossed from time to time she had always been carefully polite, calling him Mr. Grover and being on her best behavior.

Virginia was to a certain extent spoiled. Her blonde beauty had attracted every man she met, but none of them had remotely interested her until Bryce Austin suddenly appeared in the country.

She looked at him now, standing before her in the narrow hotel lobby, and experienced again that breathless eagerness which she had known when she had first seen him. No matter what this man should do she could neither resist him nor for long feel anger toward him.

"He can't be dead." She said this more to herself than to the lawyer. "Not Gilbert Grover. He can't be dead."

Long ago Bryce Austin had taken the measure of this girl whom he intended to marry. He knew her weaknesses and her strong points. He had studied her as thoroughly as he had ever studied an antagonist in a courtroom battle.

Not that he did not love her in his own way; but Austin was not a man who would ever lower his guard completely to anyone.

"He's dead." He said it gently but with a note of finality. "He tried to run Ray Pinker off the half-section of land that Ernie Sylvester is filing on, and Ray wouldn't run."

She twisted her fingers, a little dazed, trying to readjust her thinking. "Bryce, when will all of this end?"

He knew what she meant. Basically she did not approve of the action her father had taken in splitting away from the Rocking Chair, and if her father alone were involved Virginia might well swing back, her loyalties and her sympathy going to Judy Grover and Vance Clark. For Virginia feared her father but had never respected him.

Yet Austin was confident that he could control her, that she would believe any interpretation which he put upon any idea or event.

He said, "I can't see how it can actually last much longer. Even before Grover died the Rocking Chair had no chance to survive. Most of the crew went with your father, as they should have done. After all, your father made the ranch what it was, and if old Grover had had any sense he would have sold out when he had the chance."

She spoke with a trace of bitterness. "I wish Father had never started this. I wish he'd left things as they were."

"Don't blame your father," Bryce Austin could be very persuasive when he chose. "You've got to see things from his angle. For years he carried the whole ranch operation on his back, with no help from Grover."

"It was Gilbert Grover who gave him his first chance."

Austin came closer and took hold of both her arms just above the elbows. He held her thus, his fingers gripping enough so that she could feel the pressure, yet not tightly enough to hurt her.

"Do you honestly believe that your father wouldn't have gotten ahead without Gilbert's help?"

Since he was nearly a head taller than she, his nearness made her look up at him. It was a trick he used purposely, to put her at a slight disadvantage.

She shook her head. "No, I don't. My father would have gotten ahead somehow, somewhere."

"He carried Grover for a lot of years. He doubled the value of the ranch. Certainly he carried out his part of the bargain. But a man has to keep growing, Ginnie, and Gilbert Grover didn't want the operation to get any larger. He was content to sit in his easy chair and let another man earn his living for him."

Everything he said was true, and she wanted desperately to believe him. "But Judy, and Vance Clark. They'll probably go on fighting."

He pulled her against him and held her tight. "I know how you feel about them," he said tenderly. "In many ways this whole thing is harder on you than anyone else. You were raised with them. They were practically brother and sister to you."

She sighed.

"And I know that it was you who went out on the lake and rescued Clark and that fool Joe Spain."

She stirred in his grasp and tried to free herself, but his arms only tightened.

"I was proud of you." His tone warmed with emotion. No one in the world could sound more sincere than Bryce Austin when he chose. This was the quality on which he traded. It was this quality which he hoped might some day lead him to the governor's mansion in Carson City, and from there to the Senate chambers in Washington.

His plans had been laid carefully. He was busy trying to make Petry Munger the most powerful rancher in the state, figuring that once this power was his Munger would gladly help elect his future son-in-law to the governorship.

Virginia still struggled faintly against this charm. "I wish I could believe that, Bryce. I've been trying to believe it. But you were there. You could have stopped them."

He pulled back a little as if offended. "Did you ever try to stop your father from doing anything? Did you ever get in the way of Ernie Sylvester, or of the gunmen he's hired? I argued, and Sylvester suggested that they set me afoot along with Clark. Don't forget that Joe Spain had tried to pull a gun. Don't forget that he'd have killed Petry if he could."

She nodded. She did not doubt that Joe Spain had tried to kill Petry.

"And don't forget that they're the ones who have caused trouble from the first. When Grover took your father in as a partner he needed help — and he said full partner. Naturally Petry thought he meant the land holdings as well as the cattle. We've tried to fight honestly all along, but Vance Clark is too hotheaded. He tried to beat me up in the corridor at the State House, and you know that when he got back here he purposely sought me out at the Palace and renewed the quarrel."

Yes, she well remembered her own effort to keep Clark from going to the saloon.

"I'm sorry Gilbert Grover is dead. At least he was not a firebrand. He had some common sense, which is more than I can say for Vance Clark."

Deep within her she knew that she should rise to Vance's defence, but she remained quiet, still under the spell of the man before her.

"So I'm going to suggest something to you. I'm going to ask you to ride out to the Rocking Chair and talk to Judy Grover. If she will listen to anyone in the world it should be you. You're as near a sister as she ever had."

Virginia nodded again, weakly.

"Tell her you're shocked by her father's unnecessary death. Tell her you'll do anything within your power to prevent further unnecessary bloodshed. Tell her you'll force your father to pay her within reason anything she asks for the ranch. Make her see that she has no chance to win a range war — and that if she wants to save Vance Clark's life she'd better sell out."

"I'll do it," Virginia said, no longer a passive listener. "We've to keep Vance from going on the warpath. We've got to."

She pulled away abruptly, hurrying upstairs for her riding clothes.

Bryce Austin watched her go. He drew a cigar from his pocket, lit it and puffed thoughtfully until she came down stairs again. He walked with her to the livery stable and helped her mount. Then, as she rode down Elkhead's main street, he climbed the dusty stairs to his own office.

Petry Munger had been standing at the full-length window looking down upon the street. Since leaving the Rocking Chair, Munger had been living at the hotel and using the lawyer's office as a headquarters.

"How'd she take it?"

Bryce Austin removed his hat and hung it carefully on the tree. He shucked out of his long-tailed black coat and placed it meticulously on a hanger. He was fastidious about his appearance, and Munger annoyed him with his sloppy ways.

"You might shave," he said with a trace of irritation as he sat down in the desk chair.

Petry Munger ran his fingers through his three-day growth of beard and grinned slyly. "I'm no lady's man like you, Bryce."

"You can repeat that, twice," Bryce Austin told him. "Even your daughter can't stand the sight of you."

Petry Munger laughed. He was in a thoroughly good humor. Bryce Austin watched him without appearing to. Deep underneath his careful exterior Austin felt nothing but contempt for this loud-mouthed man, but he was enough of a realist to know that in this tough land Petry Munger was the type which forced itself to the top and stayed there. Austin was well aware of his own limitations. He did not belong in the desert, and the natives were inclined to view him with suspicion, even when they feared his quick legal brain. If he hoped to go anywhere in local politics he would need Munger behind him, supporting him, pushing him upward.

Munger came over and sat down on the table beside the desk, shoving a pile of papers out of his way with unthinking carelessness. The gesture increased Austin's irritation but he masked it.

"Ginnie's riding out to talk to the Grover girl," he said. "I haven't much hope of what she'll accomplish with Judy. Judy hates her guts."

Munger was honestly surprised. "Why, I thought they liked each other."

The lawyer shrugged. "I wonder you can play poker, Petry. You're such a damn poor judge of human nature. Judy's jealous of Ginnie and always has been — of her looks, and the way she attracts men, everything."

"Then why in hell did you send her out there?"

"To talk to Clark, you fool. He's in love with her, in case you haven't figured that out. Half your old crew was in love with her, but Vance had it worse than most. If Clark can be talked to by anyone it will be her. She might, she just might, talk him into quitting."

"To hell with Clark."

Austin said slowly, "You don't know what you're talking about, Petry. You and Ernie Sylvester watched him grow up. You're used to him. You still think of him as a wild kid without much brains."

"You sound like you're afraid of him," Munger said, and grinned mockingly.

"No, not afraid." Bryce Austin spoke reflectively, as if he were measuring every word. "But I found out some time ago that only a fool underrates the man he's fighting. I have no intention of making that mistake with Vance Clark."

Petry Munger grunted. "What can he do, one man? We've got half a dozen riders in the crew who can handle a gun better than him."

"I don't know," Austin was still speaking slowly, as if thinking aloud. "But Clark isn't an average man. If I didn't know better I'd think he was at least half Indian. You can't always be sure what he's thinking. I'd feel much better if I heard that he had ridden out of the country, or that he was dead."

CHAPTER
ELEVEN

Vance Clark came into the kitchen of the Grover house to find Judy at the stove already preparing breakfast. He sat down at the table without speaking, watching the girl move between the cupboard and the stove.

She turned twice to look at him. There was no sign of grief on her small face and her actions were flatly matter of fact. The events of the previous day might never have happened.

She placed the stack of cakes before him, filled his cup from the big pot and sat down. "Don't you think we'd better do some planning?"

He began cutting into the cakes. "What kind of planning?"

"What we're going to do about the ranch."

He said, "The cattle are all up on the mountain. They can't stray as long as the hot weather holds so I don't have to worry about them right now. Petry's crew is cutting the hay in the meadows, so I don't need to worry about that."

She said tartly, "You sound like a man who doesn't have too much on his mind."

He took his time chewing and swallowing. Then he said, "I spent half the night figuring where I'd go it I were Ray Pinker. I don't think he'll head back for town right away. Lem Stewart made it pretty plain yesterday that he'd arrest him on sight, and I don't think either Petry or Bryce Austin is quite ready to tangle with the sheriff yet. He can't cross the dry lake in any comfort. Maybe he could make it during the night, but I doubt it. I think he's on North Mountain."

She watched him pour on more molasses.

"Look at it from their angle." He was speaking not so much to her as he was arguing with himself. "They know we haven't any crew. They can guess that I won't be riding much across the mountain. Therefore the safest place for Pinker to hide will be up around Joetree's place. They don't like us very well up there."

She stirred faintly. He went on eating.

"I'm not going blind," he said. "I'll see if I can pick up Ray's sign and trail him up, but my hunch still holds. He'll be somewhere around Joetree's."

She rose suddenly and came around the table. She put one small hand on his shoulder and he looked up, startled.

"Why, Judy!"

"Maybe I'd better sell the ranch, Vance. Surely Petry would pay something to be rid of us."

He was taken aback. The thought had not occurred to him.

"I didn't sleep much last night either. I lay awake thinking. It isn't fair to put you into this spot. Father took an unfair advantage in asking you to stand by the ranch, asking you —" her voice broke for the barest instant — "to marry me."

He got up and took both her small shoulders between his big hands. "Judy."

She met his eyes with an effort.

"The marriage part is worrying you, isn't it?"

She nodded.

"Forget it. Your father meant well and I know why he did it — to make sure I stayed here and helped you. Well, don't worry. I'll stay, and I don't need to be married to you or to have half the Rocking Chair either. You couldn't get me out of this country with wild horses — not until I've found Ray Pinker and forced the real story of your father's death out of him. I'm going to make him crawl. I'm going to make him admit that Petry Munger hired him to shoot your father."

He let her go and walked to the door. "You might put some jerky and biscuits and coffee in a bag," he said. "I may be riding for quite a spell." And then he left.

For a while Judy stood pensively beside the table. She knew him too well to argue with his decision, yet the feeling grew within her that he was riding out onto the mountain to be killed.

She did not cry. She began preparing the food pack. When it was ready she stepped outside in time to see him cinch the saddle in place and swing up.

He rode toward her, taking the pack and fastening it behind the saddle. Then with a wordless nod he rode out of the yard.

Judy Grover stood still, oppressed by a sense of being utterly alone. It was in a manner a delayed reaction, as though until this moment the impact of her father's death had not struck her fully. She sat down on the step, looking at the wide yard and the mountain rising behind it without really seeing either.

She sat there a long time. Finally she rose and moved through the house to her father's room, settling her small body into the chair before the table desk and staring at the rows of stuffed birds which stared back at her glassily from their shelves. Then she lowered her head and for the first time since her father died, she let the tears come.

Afterward she could not recall how long she had sat there. The sound of a horse coming into the yard disturbed her, and then she heard light steps upon the porch and Virginia's voice calling,

"Judy, Judy, where are you?"

For a moment Judy Grover sat frozen, then a quick rush of deep, unreasoning anger lifted her to her feet. She caught the table and steadied herself, standing still until she could speak clearly.

"In here," she said. "In Father's office."

She heard the other girl come along the hall, and when Virginia appeared in the doorway she managed to drop her mask in place.

"It's nice of you to come," she murmured, and inside she still felt frozen. It was as if the frost sheathed the hatred which she had always felt for the other girl.

It seemed to Judy that her dislike ran back to that first day when Virginia had come to the ranch. Virginia was older by two years, and large for her age, and she had ordered Judy about with the cruelty which all children sometimes show to their juniors.

As far as Judy knew, Virginia always had been unconscious of the resentment she roused in the younger girl. She had been kind, at times too kind, and when they grew old enough for dances she had made a point of taking Judy with her, almost forcing one and then another of her numerous admirers to escort the ranch owner's daughter.

Virginia was coming across the room now, her hands outstretched, her blue eyes soft with unshed tears. "I just heard, this morning." She put her arms about Judy and pulled her close. "I —" her voice broke and Judy knew that she was crying.

Judy broke Virginia's grip as gently as she could and stepped back.

"Tears never solved anything, Ginnie. Don't waste them on me."

The older girl stopped crying, but her voice was still husky. "But Judy. What are you going to do?"

"I'll get along."

"I never understood you." Virginia was almost wailing. "Even as a little girl you never acted like other people."

And I understood you only too well, Judy thought bitterly. I always have. You never in your life looked beneath the surface, or tried to reason out what makes other people as they are. You took things at face value and enjoyed yourself. You aren't really selfish, for to be selfish you must know the meaning of the word, and you never did. You never in your life actually wondered whether the people around you were as happy as you were.

Aloud she said, "Thank you for coming, Ginnie."

"I wanted to help. I wanted to ask about the funeral . . ."

"There will be no funeral. We buried him last night."

"But Judy — that isn't civilized."

"Civilized." In spite of herself Judy's temper slipped. "Was it civilized for Ray Pinker and Ernie Sylvester to murder him?"

"Now, Judy, listen." The distress in Virginia's tone was very plain. "I know how you feel but —"

"You know how I feel?" Judy said. "How could you know? Has your father been murdered? Have your hay fields been stolen? Has the ranch that has been in your family for three generations been split and threatened?"

Virginia stared at her. She had seen Judy in tantrums as a child, but she had never seen her like this.

She said, "I'm only trying to help. I'm only trying to prevent further bloodshed."

"You'd better try. Vance rode out three hours ago."

"You mean he's gone already?"

"What did you expect — that he would sit here like a target, waiting until your father's hired killers rode up into the yard and gunned him down?"

"Judy!" Virginia Munger was growing impatient. "I can't help you unless you get a grip on yourself."

"I've got a grip on myself." Judy almost spat the words. "If I didn't have I'd drive you off the place with a whip. I don't know what you came out here for. I don't know why you don't stay on your own side of the fence."

The older girl made a little helpless gesture with her hands. "I didn't start this fight, Judy. I didn't approve of a lot of the things that were done. You were always the best friend I had. Do you think I like to see you hurt?"

Judy said nothing. She realized that Virginia was telling the truth. Virginia undoubtedly did consider Judy her best friend. Virginia honestly believed that she had always been more than kind to Judy.

"I'm only trying to help you," Virginia said. "Don't you know that I was the one who rode out onto the dry lake and saved Vance and Joe Spain?"

"You'd better go." All the fire had gone from Judy, leaving her dull and tired. "Forget what I said. Just go and leave me alone."

At once Virginia softened. "I can't. Not until I say what I came to say. You can't carry on here alone. You haven't got a crew. You'll have no winter feed. I'll make Father buy you out. I'll make him give you a fair price."

"So that's it. So your father is using you to try to trick me into selling."

"It isn't. Father had nothing to do with it. He doesn't even know I'm out here. He'd have forbidden me to come if he'd known. Bryce Austin suggested it. Bryce doesn't want blood-shed any more than I do."

The mention of the lawyer rekindled Judy Grover's anger, but she managed to say calmly, "The Rocking Chair is not for sale. Not as long as I live, or Vance Clark lives."

Virginia's voice sharpened. "Don't you think you should talk to Vance about that? After all, I doubt that anyone will take a shot at you, but they won't hesitate to shoot at him."

The younger girl stared at her. "Do you think Vance would listen to me?"

"I think he'll listen to me," Ginnie Munger said with confidence. "He always has." And was utterly unprepared for the reaction which her words caused.

"You leave him alone, Ginnie Munger!"

"Leave him alone? What are you talking about?"

Judy Grover caught the older girl's arm with both hands, shaking her. "You hear me. Leave him alone! Haven't you done enough to Vance Clark?"

"Done enough to him?"

"You led him on. I watched you for years, playing fast and loose with him like a fisherman holding a trout at the end of a line. You kept him around as long as you had any use for him, and then when your fancy Eastern lawyer came along you kicked Vance aside."

"Judy —"

"Don't you Judy me. I've watched you for years, Virginia Munger. I know more about you than you know about yourself, and I don't like one thing at all. Not one single thing about you."

"Judy, that's not true. I didn't lead Vance on."

"I suppose you're going to say that you didn't even know he was in love with you."

"Well —" She hesitated. "I knew he was fond of me, but —"

"But you were too busy thinking of yourself and of your own feelings to give any thought to how he might feel."

"I can't help it if people like me —"

"Stop it."

The older girl was watching intently. "Why, Judy — you're in love with him yourself. You never said anything. I never guessed —"

"Stop it." Judy's color had come up richly. "Stop it."

"But I —"

"Get out of here and don't come back. Don't ever set foot on the Rocking Chair again."

CHAPTER
TWELVE

Vance Clark had ridden directly toward Stinking Water from the ranch, taking the shortest trail which led across the rising shoulder of North Mountain.

He did not hurry, for he knew that the chase on which he was starting probably would not end this day or the next, or even the next. Ray Pinker had been on the Rocking Chair payroll for two years before the break between Petry and Gilbert Grover, and during that period Vance had had full opportunity to observe the man.

He came down the canyon carefully until he could see the pole line of the new fence which stretched across the upper boundary of Ernie Sylvester's claim.

Dismounting, he left his horse behind a clump of grease-wood brush and moved downward looking for sign. He found it without difficulty, where the shod hoofs of a passing horse had knocked the thin soil from the underlying rocks. He turned back, following the track as it angled across the canyon bottom and disappeared up a side draw.

He got his horse and followed, still not hurrying. The tracks were a good twenty hours old. Ray Pinker might have crossed the mountain and already disappeared in the maze of sand sinks to the northward, but Vance Clark did not believe so.

The track took him up the length of the side draw, and long sliding marks told plainly how Pinker's mount had struggled to crest out at the top of the rise.

As he climbed, the mountain loomed before Clark. It was in reality three mountains, three individual peaks of one huge jutting rock which rose from the high plateau some four thousand feet above the sand spread out at its feet, a million acres of ridges and funneled canyons, some so steep that it was a wonder cattle could feed across their faces. To the casual observer it did not seem that the canyon could support any life, but the rich bunch grass was the best feed in the world, and the Rocking Chair stock had grown sleek and multiplied upon it for the last fifty years.

"On the mountain" was an old ranch expression. The Rocking Chair crew had used it, meaning that they were riding the high crests, checking on the stock, making certain that the springs were clean, that the wooden tanks which caught the precious water were not fouled.

From his earliest memory Vance Clark had enjoyed being on the mountain. It had given him a sense of well being, a sense of freedom. A man was alone on the mountain, alone with the wind and the blue arch of the almost cloudless sky. A man was alone, even if other riders were within a mile or two of him, for the country was so rough and broken that it was hard to see for more than a few hundred feet until you crested out on

108

the bowl-like tip which nestled between the three sentinel peaks.

Ray Pinker's tracks followed a deer trail, dipping here and there to cross some small side canyon, but climbing, always climbing.

At midafternoon Vance Clark halted beside one of the lower springs, sitting slack in the saddle as he studied the marks stamped into the wet earth around the tank. There was a carpet of cattle tracks; the clean-cut holes left by half a dozen deer; larger, flatter tracks of wild burros; a lion pad, surprising by its size — a record of life which existed in this wilderness — and over them all, leading directly to the water, the heavy track of a shod horse.

At the tank's edge Pinker had stepped down, and his hand prints were plain where he had lowered himself almost to his belly to drink the cold water. Afterward he had walked away, leading the horse to the shade of a few wind twisted cedars where he had eaten, squatting on the ground.

Clark had his own lunch then, and rode again upward, losing the tracks finally as they crossed a rock slide. This did not worry him too greatly. He had convinced himself of one thing. Ray Pinker was on the mountain, and sooner or later he would find the man. It was merely a question of time and of searching.

At four o'clock the slanting sun was nearly down to the line of the sharp peaks as he dropped into the shelf-like trace which marked the line of the old mine road.

In the early seventies copper had been discovered on the mountain, and a quarter of a million investors' dollars had gone into making the road over which slow moving ox teams had hauled the rich ore to the smelter a hundred miles away.

The mine had played out, and the ox teams with their high yokes and tinkling bells were near forgotten. But the road still remained, caved in spots, at places almost blocked with rocks, yet still passable for the burro teams which brought the scant supplies up from Elkhead to Dark Rock, nestling in its sharp canyon just below the high rim.

He turned up the road and his horse increased its pace, relieved to find itself again upon the semblance of a trail. The sun dropped lower, the shadow stretched out, closing in across the bottom of the canyon and seeming to rise like a dark tide until it crossed the road he traveled.

It was near full dark before he came around the sharp bend and saw the half-dozen yellow lights that marked Dark Rock flickering at him through the gathering haze.

Once this had been a town of nearly a thousand people, supported by the copper mine whose tunnels ran a mile into the canyon side. But now only a few of the old buildings were still occupied, the rest sway-roofed and crumbling, canted at crazy angles along the canyon's rising sides.

He rode on, coming into what had been the town's main street. Side thoroughfares had climbed upward on both wings of the cut which nature had made in the

110

mountain rock, but these side streets were now brush covered, caved and littered with stones fallen from above.

The north end of the hotel porch had sagged as its underpinning gave away until it sloped at a forty degree angle, one of its posts jutting out across the ancient hitchrack.

There were no horses at the rack, and no one on the dark street as Vance Clark stepped from the saddle. He tied his mount, crossed the drooping porch and came gingerly into the old barroom.

Only one of the swinging lamps was lighted, and the big room had but four occupants. Three of them played poker at one of the rear tables and Joetree leaned on his own bar, watching the door.

He was a big man, run to fat, but even the layers of lard could not conceal the powerful frame and heavy muscles. His sleeves were rolled, and he leaned forward half across the scarred bar, his arms looking as large and as hairy as a bear's.

His face was very full and wattles ran down to almost hide his chin line. His nose was large, but his mouth was startlingly small, and he had a habit of pursing it which gave him something of a baby look.

Only his eyes moved as Vance came in. He offered no greeting, no sign of welcome, and the feeling of unwelcome, almost of hostility, persisted throughout the dusty room as if all four men were hating the intruder.

Vance Clark crossed directly to stand in front of Joetree and rest his hands upon his side of the bar as he

111

turned to give the three card players a long, careful, raking stare.

He knew how little liked the Rocking Chair was in this dying town, and he returned the opinion heartily. Without being able to prove it he had known for years that the handful of men who still grubbed in the old mine, taking out their occasional ton of ore for its gold and silver content only, ignoring the copper which had made the mine so rich, helped themselves freely to Rocking Chair beef.

But there was little either he or the rest of the crew had been able to do about it in the old days, for although North Mountain was considered Rocking Chair range it was in reality government land on which any man had the right to file and work a mineral claim.

He turned back, facing Joetree, and the man said in his curiously high voice, "Kind of off your beat, aren't you, Vance?"

Clark's shrug could have meant anything.

"Hear you and Petry Munger are having a mite of trouble." There was malice in Joetree's eyes, and the three card players at the rear table had given up all pretense of interest in their game. Vance Clark knew he was being baited, and he marveled at how much difference the Rocking Chair split had made.

In the old days Joetree and the rest of Dark Rock's sorry citizens had walked softly whenever any of the ranch crew came to town.

He said calmly, "We're having trouble. Gimme a drink, have one yourself and give the others one." He jerked his head toward the men at the card table.

Joetree's actions were studiedly deliberate. He set a single glass upon the bar and put a bottle beside it. "None of us feels like drinking," he said, and the malice burned brighter in his eyes.

Vance Clark moved as slowly as the fat man had. He reached out with his left hand and caught the front of Joetree's shirt. The fat man straightened, straining against the pressure which Vance was using in an effort to drag him across the bar. Their strengths were about equal, but the shirt's wasn't. It had been washed too many times. It parted with a loud ripping noise, splitting down the fat man's back. But Vance did not release his hold. He gave it an extra jerk, tearing it free of the collar and pulling it forward so that the rolled up sleeves hauled Joetree's arms together. Then, still holding the shirt with his left hand, he deliberately drove his right fist into Joetree's prominent nose.

The fat man yelled. A chair slammed over at the card table and Jonas Garbo was on his feet. Vance let go of Joetree's shirt and swung half around. The gun at his hip suddenly appeared in his hand and his face had a tight, pinched look.

"You want some of this, Jonas?"

Garbo's hand had closed around his gun, but he never lifted it from the holster. He froze beside the table, a colorless man in faded clothes, his mouth a little open to show his crooked, discolored teeth.

Slowly he let his hand fall away from the gun. Slowly he squatted back to retrieve his chair and slowly he slid into it. His eyes never left Vance's tight face. He seemed to find something fascinating in the fixed expression.

113

Vance looked at them with deep contempt. "You're a bunch of rats," he said. "You hide here in the hills, and grub at the leavings in the mine, and eat Rocking Chair beef."

No one answered him. Joetree had managed to free his arms of the remains of his shirt and was using it to dab at his nose, which was bleeding copiously.

"All right," Vance said. "You hate me, and you hate the Rocking Chair, because in some twisted way you blame us for your troubles. But let me tell you something. If it hadn't been for Gilbert Grover, Petry Munger would have run you off the mountain years ago."

They stared at him.

"Gilbert Grover is dead. Ray Pinker killed him and Ray's on the mountain somewhere, probably right here in town. I want him. I'm going to get him, and it will be better for all of you if you help me."

Joetree had stopped dabbing at his nose. Joetree said in his high, whining voice, "You've got a strange way of trying to make friends, Vance. You play a little rough."

Vance Clark turned on him a contempt he made no effort to hide. "There are only two things you thieves understand, and friendship isn't either of them. You either laugh at a man or you crawl to him. Now, start crawling. Where's Ray Pinker?"

"Never heard of him."

Clark balanced the gun in his hand as if trying to make sure whether or not it was heavy enough for his purpose. He seemed to decide that it was.

"Come out from behind that bar."

114

Joetree watched him. The men at the back table watched him. He could almost feel the intensity of their collective gaze as it burned its way through his shirt.

"Come out." The gun steadied. Its muzzle leveled at the mat of hair which covered Joetree's big chest.

The man swore at him. He came slowly along the bar to the break, like an unwilling, grouchy dog which minds its master through fear rather than through love.

"Get down on your knees," Vance Clark said.

Joetree stared at him through eyes which were crystal with disbelief. Joetree had ruled Dark Rock with a heavy hand, bossing the brush jumpers and petty rustlers who made the old town their headquarters.

In his own slow way he was proud of his position and his power, and he knew clearly that once he crawled to Vance Clark's feet that power would be gone.

"Hell with you," he said.

The gun in Vance's hand seemed to explode of its own volition. The heavy bullet cut a neat round hole in the scuffed floor directly between Joetree's booted feet. The big man stared downward at the hole as if he did not quite believe it. Then he spoke in a dry, husking voice.

"He's up at the old mine, in the shaft house. He came in here last night."

Vance Clark watched Joetree. He did not doubt the man's words. He knew almost instinctively why Joetree had cracked. It was not the shot, or even the fear of being shot. It was the fear of being broken before his own men.

And yet, he had still been broken. By telling Vance Clark where Ray Pinker was hiding he had accepted defeat. It was not that Pinker meant anything to Joetree, or to the castoffs who made their home in this rotting camp. But Pinker was outside the law and the law was their natural enemy, and once they surrendered to it they were finished.

Vance said quietly, "I'm going after him. Anyone I see move on the canyonside will get shot."

He turned then and went out into the darkness of the street. Behind him there was not a single sound from the room he had just left. He stopped beyond the edge of the shadowed porch, knowing that there were other men in the dark night, probably drawn from their holes by the sound of his shot.

Yet it was characteristic of the place that they remained within the darkness, not stepping forward into the light, for their caution was stronger than their curiosity.

He moved silently across the dust, aware of each whisper in the night. There was no moon, and the star studded sky could be seen only through the aperture between the canyon's upflung wings. Only a little light filtered down into the street, and this was somehow lost so that the shadows which the old buildings made seemed deeper because of its faint glow.

He had the sensation, as he always did in Dark Rock, that a thousand ghosts watched his progress, ghosts of the men who had once labored here, who had turned the gulch into an echoing bedlam with the noise of their revelries.

The town had still held some of its life during his early boyhood, and had been a favorite place for the Rocking Chair's crew to knock off their boredom with their Saturday night invasions; but that life had trickled away during the ten years to leave the canyon dark and sullen, a place of suspicion, of resentment and of shattered hopes.

He climbed the rising grade of the street until he saw above him the spider-like web of the old tramway which had carried a hundred swinging buckets, lowering the ore from the high mine to the waiting ox teams below.

The cable still stretched its sagging length, but the buckets had fallen to lie rusting in the brush which nature thrust up in a valiant effort to obscure the damage men had wrought to the earth's crust.

He almost stumbled over one of them, and then he reached the swelling line of the old dump, a high, man-made hump across the canyonside where the miners had spilled their thousands of tons of worthless rock.

He climbed. The dump was so old, and had stood so many winters, that it was packed nearly as solidly as the natural canyon walls.

He made as little noise as possible, but in the darkness it was a tricky climb. More than once his foot dislodged a stone not as well rooted as its fellows, to send it crashing down to the floor of the dark gulch.

Above him the ruined shaft house with its rotting head-frame loomed against the lighter sky, and as he breasted one shoulder of the dump and came about the corner of the sagging sorting shed he saw the flicker of light within.

He had no doubt that the light belonged to Ray Pinker, and he moved more carefully now, using his hands on the sloping sides to steady his advance, creeping forward, making each step an individual action of its own until he came up to the rough boards of the shack.

The door had long since fallen from its hinges, and someone had hung a tattered blanket to mask the opening. He paused outside, took a deep breath, drew the gun from its holster and pushed the blanket to one side.

Ray Pinker lay on a pile of other blankets in the far corner, asleep. It was evident that he had dozed unintentionally, for he had not even pulled off his boots or blown out the lantern.

Vance Clark stepped into the room. One of the old boards creaked under his shifting weight. Pinker stirred and started to sit up, his eyes still blurred with sleep. "That you, Ernie?"

"Get up," Clark said.

Pinker raised on one elbow, blinking owlishly in the light.

"Get up and be careful."

The man swung his feet to the floor, sitting stiffly on the edge of the bunk. His holstered gun was hanging by its belt from a peg in the wall. He looked at it as if calculating his chances.

"Don't try it. All I want is an excuse to kill you."

Ray Pinker stood up, looking curiously shrunken. "Vance, listen."

"I don't want to hear it, Ray. You killed one of the few decent men I've ever known."

"But I didn't." The words were almost a wail. "I didn't shoot Gil Grover. Ernie did."

Vance Clark used the back of his hand to wipe his mouth. "Don't lie, Ray."

"I'm not lying." Pinker sounded desperate. "You've got to believe me. I was building fence when Gil rode up. He sat there holding his rifle on me. He told me to pull the wire down and dig out the posts. There was a shot, and Ernie came running toward us. The bullet knocked Gil off his horse, but it didn't kill him. He made a rush for the canyon wall and started to climb —"

"You'll have to tell a better story than that."

"I can't." Ray Pinker sounded hopeless, as if he realized that nothing he would say would do any good, that death was standing here with him in this rotting mine shack.

Something in his very hopelessness made Vance say, "All right. Tell me the rest. Why did you run?"

"I didn't. I was hiding in the brush while you talked to Ernie, while the others rode up. After you took Gil's body Petry talked to me. He didn't want Ernie accused. The homestead is in Ernie's name. He offered me a thousand dollars gold to drift out of the country. I've been waiting for it to be sent up here."

"Come on. Bring the lantern."

"Where are we going?"

"Down to Elkhead, to tell your story to the sheriff."

Pinker wet his lips. "I —"

"It's either that or die here."

Pinker hesitated. Then he sighed gustily and picked the lantern from the peg and started for the doorway. As he stepped into it a shot hammered from the dump. He stopped. The lantern dropped to the ground and smashed, extinguishing itself.

Ernie Sylvester's high yell rang through the night.

"That was Pinker. Vance must still be inside."

CHAPTER
THIRTEEN

The shot caught Vance entirely unprepared, but his instinctive reaction carried him backward across the room to where the old haulage tunnel opened in the far wall like the gaping mouth of a cave.

In the darkness his boot heel caught on the rusty rail which had once carried the loaded ore car from the mine to the chutes through which the bucket line was filled.

He fell heavily, and the act probably saved his life, for outside half a dozen guns exploded as if on some given signal, the heavy slugs tearing their way through the weathered planks of the shack's walls.

There was a shout from the dump, another volley, and then in the sudden weighted silence the sound of Ernie Sylvester's voice.

"All right. Two of you rush the door. We'll cover you."

Vance was on his hands and knees, crawling over the wet roughness of the ties which supported the mine's rails. A good two inches of ice cold water ran down the tunnel's floor, and it soaked him as he scrambled into the blackness beyond.

There was a twist in the tunnel a hundred feet back from the entrance as the drift made an angular turn following the vein, and he ran almost head-on into the rotting timbering of the wall. He caught himself and staggered.

Behind him came a confused mutter of shouts and then the flare of a match. He moved around the bend, splashing in the shallow water, and drew a shot which struck the wall behind him, thudding wetly into the soggy planking.

Beyond the corner he paused to draw a long, tortured breath. He could hear the rumble of their excited voices behind him, but the walls of the tunnel and the water combined to give the sounds an eerie quality, as though they issued from another world.

And then suddenly there came a quick rush of panic. It was something Vance had never experienced before, something he did not understand. He had been afraid at times of course — only a fool, a man with no imagination has ever escaped fear — but always his fear had been tempered by the knowledge of the strength within himself, of his ability to meet most situations.

But here he was blocked, caught underground, by half a dozen men who had nothing on their minds except to find the way to bring about his death.

In this whole mouldering town there was not one person whom he could call a friend, not one man whom he might reasonably expect would give him aid. He was trapped alone, in the darkness, threatened not only by their guns but by the fact that the timber was rotten, that the moisture had for years eaten at the standing rock walls, so that at any second they might give way and cave in.

His first impulse was to call out, offering to surrender, to walk back out of the tunnel with his hands raised. But reason quelled the urge quickly. He could expect no mercy from Ernie Sylvester, no chance of life from the Double M crew.

He turned, moving cautiously so that he would make as little noise as possible. In the water he felt his way along the tunnel wall, deeper and deeper into the hill.

He had traveled over a hundred yards when his groping fingers encountered the rungs of a rising ladder. He had no idea where it led. The blackness above him was intense and he dared not strike a match.

He paused, listening, and behind him, near the tunnel's mouth he heard the splash of slowly moving feet and caught the distant glint of a light.

They had found a lantern. They were coming in after him. He climbed, spurred upward by the danger of their approach, yet he took time before trusting his weight to each new rung to test its strength, only transfering his full pressure when he was certain that it would bear him.

Three times the cross pieces broke under him, and once he only saved himself from falling by grasping the ladder's uprights and dangling while he scrambled for footing.

But he reached the top finally, forty feet above the tunnel floor, and climbed up through what seemed to be a hole cut vertically into the solid rock.

Here he stopped, fumbled a match from his pocket and risked striking it.

He was in a room-like opening, perhaps twenty feet wide and nearly fifty feet long, which had been stoped out along the vein.

The hole through which he had struggled was an ore chute, left for the purpose of sliding the broken quartz down into the tunnel he had just left.

He stood at the rim peering downward, seeing the waver of light below as his pursuers moved gingerly along the rails, their progress marked by the splashing in the shallow water. Then he turned away along the length of the stope.

There was a weirdness about being chased underground as if he were a mole and his pursuers ferrets, but his first panic had faded.

He lit a second match and by its meager light found a second rise with a ladder leading upward. Climbing this, he came into a second stope. The vein had apparently pitched at an angle toward the south, so that the foot wall slanted upward as he walked on an incline of nearly thirty degrees.

He climbed again and yet again, until he had entirely lost his sense of direction. The forgotten miners seemed to have gutted the whole mountain, leaving pillars and floor between the rooms to support the rock roofs.

It was hot in the upper rooms, and the deadness of the air made breathing difficult. He paused, listening, wondering if he could ever find his way out, even if the Double M crew were not there waiting for him.

124

He lit another match. The darkness made the dead air doubly oppressive, and in the tiny flame he saw yet another ladder leading upward from the far end of this stope. The match burned down until it singed his fingers, and he dropped it in the dust of the uneven floor.

Then he groped his way forward along the sharp rock edges of the wall until he reached the ladder and climbed slowly. Before he reached the top he became conscious of a downdraft of fresher air. He climbed faster, fighting down an excitement which ran through him. He came into the upper chamber and paused, peering around eagerly in the darkness. He lit another precious match. Disappointment washed over him. This room was very much like the one he had just left, except further south, since the vein continued to cant in that direction. At its end was another ore chute and another upward ladder.

He dropped the match and felt his way onward. As he reached the ladder and began to climb he was again conscious of the downdraft of fresh air. He mounted, groping his way, and came into the upper room. Again he lit a match.

This one flickered, almost going out. He cupped it in his hands and started toward the far end. Then he stopped, for instead of the ladder he saw a mound of earth, and above it in the roof, an irregular hole through which he could catch a glimpse of distant stars.

The hole, for it was little more, had been broken through onto the outcropping, probably by accident. This had been a long time ago and dirt and rubbish had fallen through, piling on the floor until it nearly reached the roof.

He scrambled onto this pile and from its top he could reach up to the edge of the broken earth. He fumbled for a handhold, found an embedded rock and began to lift himself.

He felt the rock slip and dropped back, ducking aside as it thudded to the earth beside his feet. He swore softly under his breath. To be so close, and yet so far from freedom. He thought of the ladders he had climbed, but they were all anchored solidly to the rock walls. It would be the height of irony if having come so near he failed to get out.

He remembered a story he had once heard of a man trapped by a mine cave-in, who had managed with his fingers to dig away the fallen earth and stones only to find that a huge boulder blocked his path. When rescuers finally found his body, he lay on his stomach, his nose pressed to the tiny crack between the boulder and the tunnel wall.

Vance Clark breathed deeply, and then with steady hands he produced the next to his last match. In its brief glow he examined the edges of the hole.

Ground water had washed down, cutting away the earth, leaving rocks and roots exposed. It was the roots to which he gave his attention. None was much larger than his arm, but one jutted out like a handle, both its ends buried in the rocky soil.

The match died, and in the darkness he felt above his head until his fingers found the root.

He tested it cautiously, letting more and more of his weight swing upon it until he had drawn both feet clear of the pile of rubble beneath him.

For a sickening instant it seemed to be giving, sliding, as if the small feeder roots which laced it to the ground were pulling loose. Then it held and he raised himself, chinning as on a bar, twisting his body upward until he got one booted leg clear of the hole, feeling with his heel for some support. He found it by hooking his toe around the exposed edge of a boulder and for a second he lay almost flat, his body a bridge across the hole, his head hanging downward into it.

He had time to wonder what would happen to him if the root suddenly let go, and then he rolled to safety on the rocky surface beside the hole and got slowly to his feet.

Above him the sky was a star speckled arch, and he thought nothing had ever looked so friendly or so good. He glanced downward at the irregular pattern of lights which the town made in the canyon below him, and he knew a quiet, consuming rage.

He was soaked with sweat. It was the only indication of the strain he had been under during the last half hour. He stood motionless, looking down on the old mine buildings and on the town far beneath them.

Caution advised him to turn and climb the canyon wall which still towered above him; but then he would be afoot on the mountain, miles from the ranch, without either a horse or food.

He started down, taking a diagonal course which would bring him east of the mine buildings by a good three hundred yards and drop him into the town's main street below the hotel.

Lights still showed in the mine buildings, and he wondered grimly how long Ernie Sylvester and the Double M men would pursue their hopeless search for him within the old workings.

He only hoped that they were all at the mine, that none of them had remained in the town below. He came down the canyonside, working his way carefully over the rough rocks. At places he had to climb back and try another path, since the one he had been following ended abruptly in a rock face which he could not cross.

It was harsh work, and his fingers were bleeding before he finally reached the more even slope running down into the dust of the town.

He paused here, behind some old houses which, judging by the condition of their caving roofs, were no longer occupied, and then came through their brush grown yards and out into the street. Here he stopped, staring at the sagging hitch-rail before the old hotel. His horse was no longer in sight. In fact, he did not see a single animal on the whole length of the curving roadway.

He stood frowning, caught by the unexpectedness of this further setback. The Double M riders had probably taken their own mounts as far as the foot of the dump, but where was his horse, and where were the animals which belonged to the stray riders who made the old camp their headquarters?

Slowly he started toward the hotel, staying as much in the deeper shadow as possible. He pulled his gun from its holster and spun the cylinder to make sure that dirt had not clogged it. He dropped the gun back into place and mounted the collapsing steps of the old porch.

Joetree was still behind the bar, and he saw half a dozen customers in the big room. He looked them over carefully, decided that none rode for the Double M, and pushed the door open with the heel of his left hand. He stepped into the place before anyone realized his presence.

Joetree had been talking, and his mouth stayed open.

Vance Clark said softly, "No, you aren't looking at a ghost. I'm real."

Joetree's lips came together, and the tip of his pink, rather small tongue slid out to run around their dirty circle. He said, "How'd you get out of the mine?"

Vance Clark allowed himself a thin, faint grin. "Never mind that. Just remember, Joetree, I'm hard to kill and so is the Rocking Chair. This country has to realize that, and the only way to make a pack of dogs realize something is to whip them."

Someone at the rear of the room laughed. Clark did not make the mistake of diverting his attention to the man. He said tonelessly, "As long as Gil Grover lived he wouldn't let us run you out. He's dead, and not one of you understood how much of a friend you had in him. So I'm telling you now. You're through on the mountain. You're through as of tonight."

A wicked light came up to dance in the fat man's eyes.

"You'll do well to look at your hole card, friend Vance. There's a dozen men in this town who would think nothing of shooting you in the back. They know Ernie Sylvester and Petry Munger and Bryce Austin would thank them well. You don't have a horse and you're only one man. You were a fool to come in here. You should have crept back into the hills when you could. You are, if you will pardon my saying so, a dead man. There's no way out."

"Isn't there?" Clark said, and he smiled.

Deliberately he raised his gun and sent a bullet through the glass bowl at the bottom of the big swinging lamp. It shattered, and spraying oil seemed to fill the air, dropping to the floor as the hot wick fell into a small pool which blazed up quickly to lick at the worn, dry boards.

With a startled oath Joetree jumped forward to stamp out the blaze. The bullet from Vance Clark's gun cut the floor in front of his feet.

"Keep back."

The fat man stopped. He stared at Vance Clark with eyes which were not quite sane.

"There's more than one way to drive out coyotes," Vance Clark said. He held them under his gun until he was sure the fire could not be controlled, and then he vaulted across the porch and vanished in the shadows. Behind him, one building after another caught, until the whole sorry town was burning fiercely.

130

CHAPTER
FOURTEEN

The news that Vance Clark had burned the old mining town ran through the country. Not even Gilbert Grover's death, had created more excitement. And much to the surprise of Elkhead's citizens, Cray Joetree appeared in the county seat and preferred charges against Vance Clark.

It was the first time in years that Joetree had come to town, and probably the first time in his life that he had consciously sought the attention of the law.

He sat in Lem Stewart's office, his face a curious gray, his rather shrill voice made hoarse by anger. He did not look up at the sheriff as he talked, but kept his eyes on the broken black hat which he twisted mechanically in his powerful fingers.

"Vance Clark had no cause to do it," he said. "He had no cause to burn my town."

Lem Stewart had known Joetree since the fat man's childhood and had never liked him. He spat expressively, making the battered cuspidor ring.

"You must have done something to provoke him."

"Not a thing," Joetree said. "He rode into town looking for Ray Pinker. I didn't help him, but I didn't hinder him. It wasn't my business."

The old sheriff's eyes narrowed. "I heard talk that Ernie Sylvester and some of Petry's men cornered Clark in the old mine. I even heard they shot Pinker by mistake and buried him behind the old dump."

The fat man concentrated on his hat. "I wouldn't know nothing about that. I only know my grandpap laid out that townsite when the mines was running. I know I bought up all the old buildings one by one. It was my property and I want something done."

"What?"

Bryce Austin stood at the window, his back to the room. Lem Stewart had been surprised when the lawyer appeared with Joetree. He had not been aware of their knowing each other.

Austin said, "My client wishes to swear out a warrant for Vance Clark's arrest. Arson will do for the time being. We might even think up something else. Pinker's murder, perhaps."

"Then Pinker is dead." The sheriff's tone had not changed.

Bryce Austin bit his lip, but he ignored the implications. "We also intend to start a civil suit to recover what we can for the damage Clark caused."

"So that's it," Lem Stewart said.

Bryce Austin looked at him coldly. "What do you mean by that?"

Lem Stewart spat again into the cuspidor. "I couldn't figure it, Joetree coming in here, wanting to swear out a warrant. Men like Joetree don't trouble much about warrants usually."

Bryce Austin said nothing.

132

"And I couldn't figure your coming in too, acting as Joetree's lawyer. Men like Joetree don't usually have lawyers."

"That's his privilege."

"Sure," Lem Stewart said. "It's a free country. A man can do a lot of things. But I like to know why."

"And you think you know?"

"I think I know. Under Gil Grover's will, Vance Clark gets a piece of the Rocking Chair. I have a hunch Joetree didn't come to you. As soon as you heard about the burning of the old mining camp you went to him."

"That's a pretty serious statement, Sheriff. There's a term for attorneys who go out chasing business."

The old man squinted at him. "In my book there's several terms, none of them polite. I smell Petry Munger in this."

He swung on Joetree suddenly. "How much are Munger and this Jayhawker paying you to stir up trouble for the Rocking Chair?"

Joetree looked up for the first time since entering the office, and his fat face was bland as he said, "Sheriff, I don't even rightly know what you're talking about."

"I'll tell you," Lem Stewart said. "You're starting a criminal action which will make a fugitive of Vance. You're also starting a civil action, and this very smart attorney of yours will go into court and request a restraining order, preventing Vance and Judy Grover from disposing of any property of the ranch until the suit is settled. And I'll chance another guess. Your lawyer will make very certain that the case is continued and not heard. He doesn't want you to win, Joetree.

He's only trying to tie Vance's hands until fall, when he and Petry can drive the Double M herd across the sink and move it onto North Mountain.

"I hope you're being well paid, Joetree, because I can tell you that once Petry is astraddle of North Mountain he'll have no more use for you."

Bryce Austin's handsome face flushed a shade redder and his voice hardened. "Sheriff, you are a public official. As such you are supposed to enforce the law impartially."

Lem Stewart swiveled his head toward him. "Sonny, I've been a peace officer for nearly forty years. I don't need you to tell me my business."

"Then you'll serve the papers on Vance if I get them?"

"If I can find him."

For a moment their eyes locked, then Bryce Austin jerked his thumb toward the door. "Come on, Joetree." He went out and the fat man followed him, for all the world like a trained bear.

An hour later Lem Stewart lifted his old body into the saddle and headed his horse out across the shoulder of the mountain toward the Rocking Chair. In his pocket he had a warrant for Vance Clark's arrest on the charge of maliciously burning the mining camp. With it was a notice of a civil suit between Joetree and Clark for one hundred and fifty thousand dollars, representing the estimated value of the property which had been destroyed.

In spite of himself Lem Stewart grinned at the thought of the figure which had been set. One hundred and fifty thousand dollars for a ghost town. He muttered to his horse, "I know fifty of them strung across the state that can be had for a hundred and fifty cents."

But his smile faded. This was not a joke. He also carried a court order, restraining Vance Clark and Judy Grover from disposing of any property held by them until the case was heard.

A dull, quiet rage filled Lem Stewart. He had thought that he was too old for deep anger, too calloused by his years of wearing a badge to be troubled by the injustices which often went on behind the shelter of the law.

But the operations of Bryce Austin seared through all of his defenses. He had disliked the man from his first arrival. Austin's obvious feeling of superiority had not set well with the old peace officer, nor had the newcomer's suave manners.

More than anything else, however, Austin's preëmption of Virginia Munger's affections galled Lem Stewart. The sheriff had watched Vance grow up, and he liked the boy despite the streak of wildness which sometimes had put Clark at odds with constituted authority. Along with almost everyone else in the county, the sheriff had recognized that Virginia Munger was Clark's girl.

As he rode along the trail which climbed its zigzag course across the lava flow, Lem Stewart traced the pattern of the last two years, and he realized that the change had come into the country with the arrival of Bryce Austin. First Virginia had stopped going to dances with Vance. Next, Bryce Austin had become attorney for the Rocking Chair and his engagement to the girl had been announced. And after that, there had come the break between Gilbert Grover and Petry Munger.

The sheriff speculated on the lawyer's reason for causing that break, and judged that Austin had had an innate fear of Gilbert Grover. Austin could confuse men like Petry Munger, but Gilbert Grover would worry him. The quiet man had been shrewd in his own way, and he hadn't been impressed by Austin's education and background.

The sheriff sighed. He walked his horse into the Rocking Chair yard, rode to the porch and stepped down heavily, as befitted a man who had spent more than fifty years in a saddle.

The front door opened and Judy Grover appeared.

"Why, Uncle Lem."

The sheriff removed his hat and used a blue handkerchief to wipe the moisture from his high forehead. "I swear, Judy, you get prettier by the year."

She came across the porch. "Save your blarney, Uncle Lem. You didn't ride all the way out here in this heat to tell me that."

He sighed again, climbing the three steps to stand before her. "I didn't, honey, and that's a fact. I'm here on a nasty business." He fumbled in his pocket as if half hopeful that he had lost the offending papers.

But he found them, and extended them to her silently.

She took them, her small face a grave triangle, her dark eyes serious, reminding him of her dead father. But she made no effort to examine the papers.

"Tell me what it's all about, Uncle Lem."

He gave her a small smile. "It's powerful dry, riding."

At once she was contrite. "You're probably the first person who ever rode into this ranch without being asked in. Let's get out of this sun."

She led the way into the coolness of the house, seating him in the chair which had been her father's. She brought a glass of water, cold from the olla, and then, leaning against her father's desk, she repeated, "What is it about?"

The sheriff set down the empty glass regretfully and wiped the tips of his drooping mustache. "It looks like Bryce Austin and Petry Munger are still pushing." He went on to tell her about the burning of the mining camp, trying to judge from her expression whether or not she had already heard the news. Then he told her of Joetree's suit and the warrant for Vance's arrest.

When he had finished, Judy still held the papers in her small hand, but she held them away from her, as if she were afraid that they might bite.

"It isn't fair." She said it vehemently. "Isn't the law supposed to protect people? Who started this trouble? Not Vance. Who split the ranch and murdered my father? Not Vance. Yet the men who are responsible are walking Elk-head's streets, free and untroubled, while you have a warrant for Vance's arrest."

The sheriff stirred uncomfortably. "I'm working on it, Judy. Your father's death I mean. But I need evidence."

"Evidence!" she almost snarled at him. "Have you any evidence that Vance burned that town?"

"Joetree swore out a warrant. If you want to swear out a warrant charging Petry with murdering your father I'll serve it. But if you fail to make your case in court he can sue you for false arrest."

"False arrest." Her laughter was near hysteria. "False arrest. What could he gain by that? He's taken everything I own now, everything I ever held dear. No, when I move against Petry it won't be through the law. The law I've seen is for tricksters."

The old man was troubled. Deep in his heart he had to agree that the law certainly seemed to be working on the wrong side here, but he had given his full life to upholding the written statutes and he felt that he must say something to defend the rules which men had laid down to govern themselves.

He said, "You're young, Judy, and in a sense you've been sheltered. You're coming up against life for the first time, and life is cruel."

She said steadily, "I don't know about life, but I know my father is dead and Vance is out on the mountain like some hunted animal. If Petry's men catch up with him, you don't actually believe they will bring him into court alive?"

The sheriff picked up the empty glass, studied it and put it down again.

"But they won't get him," she said fiercely. "And if they do I'll personally shoot each and every one of them. Not a single rider from the Double M will be safe, I promise you that."

138

Lem Stewart eyed her thoughtfully. "Vance means an awful lot to you, doesn't he, girl?"

"He's all I have left," she said simply.

Stewart did not carry the subject further, but he began to adjust his thinking. He had always assumed that Vance belonged to Virginia Munger. It had never occurred to him that Judy Grover was interested in Clark, and he doubted very much if Clark was conscious of the interest.

If Vance didn't return her feeling, he thought, it would hurt her worse than she had already been hurt.

Aloud he said, "I can't advise you what to do, Judy. I've got to serve you with the order restraining you from disposing of the ranch or any property which Vance might have any claim to."

"I have no intention of disposing of anything. But I'd like to know how Bryce Austin found out so soon what was in my father's will."

The sheriff nodded. "I wondered some myself, so I asked a few questions. It seems that when your father rode into town before going out to Stinking Water he stopped and left a copy of the will with Holland, the banker, for safe-keeping. Bryce Austin is attorney for the bank."

She said bitterly, "Isn't there one thing in this country that that sneak hasn't got his long fingers into?"

The sheriff shrugged.

"I don't understand it. Here we are. We've lived all our lives in this country. I hold nothing. You hold nothing. Yet Bryce Austin can come in here and in a few years make himself one of the most powerful men in the county — yes, in the state."

"Maybe most of us don't think the way he does," Lem Stewart said lamely.

"Maybe we should start —" She broke off, interrupted by the sound of a horse coming into the yard.

For a moment neither of them moved. Then Judy reached around to the desk drawer at her side and pulled out the heavy gun which Gil Grover had always kept there. It was not loaded. It had not been fired during her lifetime, but Lem Stewart did not know that.

"Judy," he said. "Judy —"

"Don't move." The heavy barrel was steady on his chest. "Don't make me kill you, Uncle Lem."

Stewart did not move. Judy raised her voice. "Vance, Vance, is that you?"

There was a faint answer.

"Get away. The sheriff is here. He has a warrant for your arrest."

In the yard there was silence, and then the quick drum of hoofs as Vance Clark rode out.

CHAPTER
FIFTEEN

From a vantage point a good half mile above the yard Vance watched Lem Stewart's departure. He was too old a hand at the ways of the country to ride down to the ranch just yet. He trusted Lem Stewart as much as he trusted any man on earth, but he also knew the sheriff thoroughly. No matter where the old man's sympathies lay Lem Stewart would never shirk his duty.

He squatted on the ridge and waited. Just when he was about convinced that Stewart had indeed headed back to town, he saw Judy leave the porch and cross to the corral.

He watched her rope a horse, saddle it and swing gracefully up, and he felt a flash of apprehension as she rode out of the yard. He had seen her ride out thus a thousand times, but never before had it seemed ominous. He searched his mind for the reason, and decided that he had never before felt responsible for her, even though he had taught her to ride.

As long as her father lived, Judy had been protected. Now, it was Judy and Vance Clark against the world.

141

She headed south and dropped out of sight in a cross canyon. Where was she heading? Already the sun was well down in the western sky. He could not imagine what Judy could be up to unless she was looking for him.

He brought his horse out of the concealing timber, mounted and dropped off the ridge, still wary, for Lem Stewart might well be lurking in the rough country to the west. He saw nothing of the sheriff as he came down to the line of the yard, so he circled it, picking up Judy's trail.

He pushed his horse, expecting as he topped each intervening rise to come within sight of her. But he did not catch her.

The print of her horse was plain, and it finally dawned on him as she continued south that she was riding toward Stinking Water.

He frowned, remembering small things which he had hardly noticed at the time. He recalled that she had been carrying her rifle when she left the house, and that she had shoved it into the boot before mounting.

This was not like Judy. At times she had carried her small caliber revolver, but he could hardly recall when she had carried a rifle.

He spurred his horse, filled suddenly with a strong foreboding. Had she decided to take the law into her own hands and ride after Ernie Sylvester?

He climbed the ridge and took the trail which led downward to the distant hot springs. The sun had dropped below the rim of the desert sink far to the west, but the light lingered. He hauled up abruptly, realizing that he had not checked her tracks for the last several miles.

The trail was not heavily traveled, and the marks he and she had made when they brought her father's body home still showed. But the tracks he had been following from the ranch were not visible.

He dismounted, scanning the scarred dust. The right front shoe of the bay she rode carried a bar which he himself had put on to protect a cracked hoof. He did not see it. He lifted himself back into the saddle and groaned. He was tired. He had gotten only an hour's sleep in some brush high above the old mining town, and he had been in the saddle for nearly nine hours.

He turned back, watching the trail-side. He retraced his route for a good three miles until he saw where Judy had swung into a side draw.

He dismounted to make sure, but her tracks, although faint, showed on the stony ground. He followed. Darkness was coming rapidly now, like a spreading blanket, filling the hollows first and then sending long fingers of its shadows creeping up the rising ground until only the peaks far above him were still bathed in the late afterglow.

He lost her track finally, but the draw continued downward and he followed it as a matter of course, realizing that it would bring him out on the bench three or four miles to the west of the hot springs.

It was full dark before he dropped low enough to see the faint yellow lights from the windows of the line camp cabin above the hay fields.

Here he halted, undecided, not knowing which way to turn. It seemed pointless to ride on. He did not know whether the girl had swerved right toward the distant town or left toward the hay camp. If she were riding for Elkhead this was certainly a roundabout way to come, and he could not think of any reason that would bring her to the hay camp unless she had some crazy notion of facing Ernie Sylvester.

He turned finally toward the distant cabin. If she had ridden toward town she would be in little danger, but at the Stinking Water anything might happen. He had covered half the distance to the cabin when something to the right of it and beyond it caught his attention. For an instant he thought it was someone moving across the freshly cut field with a lantern. Then the flickering flame spurted up and he swore hoarsely. Someone was firing one of the stacks.

The flame crawled upward, as if only half willing to ignite the cured hay. But another flame bloomed to the left, a hundred yards beyond the first. Someone was burning Petry Munger's hay. Someone named Judy Grover.

He cursed her under his breath for the chance she was taking. But he had to admit even as he put his horse into motion that Judy had chosen the one way to fight Munger on his own ground.

With the hay gone Munger lost one of his trump cards. He would be no better prepared to face the winter than Rocking Chair. And he would gain little by driving his herd across the sink from South Mountain, wearing the animals down on a three-day, feedless drive with no hay at the end of it.

A third flame flared into life. The first stack was now blazing like a huge bonfire, lighting the whole upper end of the meadow.

The men in the cabin must be seeing the light by now, and Clark shifted his attention toward the building. Any danger to the girl would come from there, and he swung his horse half around, changing his direction and jerking the rifle free of the boot.

At least he could give her this much protection, nor was he a moment too soon. As he came forward in the half light thrown up from the distant burning stacks he saw the cabin door come open.

Three men appeared. He fired. The bullet thudded into the logs above the door and a high, startled yell rose up through the night. The three men dived for the safety of the building, and the door slammed. He drove a bullet against its heavy planking as an added warning for them to hold their place indoors.

There was a rear entrance, and he knew that he could not cover both front and rear. But he had gained precious minutes and he spurred toward the huge field where a fifth stack had just burst into flame. He called Judy's name as he rode, called to let her know who it was.

Behind him a shot cracked, and then another, and he judged that the men he had driven to cover had run through the house and spilled out the rear door toward the corral. In a minute or so they would be in the saddle. He had to get Judy out of there.

He could see her plainly in the light of the burning hay. Two stacks had not yet been fired, and after a brief glance in his direction she spurred her horse at them.

He swung in the saddle and sent two fast shots after the men who were running for the corral. He did not expect to hit anyone, but in the brassy light from the leaping fires he had the satisfaction of seeing one of them hit the dust and then crawl crab-like toward the pole fence.

He swung back and rode toward Judy. She had dismounted beside one of the remaining stacks. She was having trouble with her horse. The animal had been spooked by the rising flames and the eerie light they cast.

She was still trying to quiet the horse as Clark rode up. He flung himself out of the saddle, tossed his reins to her and snatched the handful of matches from her fingers. No words passed between them. He ran to the stack, pulled out handfuls of loose hay.

His first match flared and died in the wind. Behind him he heard the pounding of horses. He forced himself to move slowly, striking the match and sheltering the little flame in his cupped hands until it caught solidly on the stick, then carefully thrusting it under the stalks of dried grass. They blazed up quickly only to fade. He pressed them closer together, against the tiny flame, and saw the matted grass catch. The fire began to spread until the flame, nearly a foot high, ate against the side of the shack.

He did not need Judy's warning shout. He turned, saw three riders pressing toward them across the stubble of the field. He made a running mount as he snatched the reins from Judy's hand. Together they swung toward the south, angling away from their pursuers as a rifle sent its flat whang across the fire-laced night.

Vance twisted in the saddle, using his forty-five to throw five quick shots above the riders' heads.

They eased their pace.

Judy was ahead of him, nearing the south edge of the field. Beyond her a strip of low brush, not sufficiently high to hide them, ran down to lose itself in the sands of the sink below. She wheeled, cutting eastward through the brush, and he realized that she was heading up the line of the ditch which led to the hot springs above.

He followed. He had no choice. Behind him the stacks were blazing pyres and the riders from the house had turned back, as if they had some vague idea of combatting the fires.

He shouted at Judy, but a good hundred yards separated them now and she apparently did not hear. They drove past the house beside the springs and into the canyon in which her father had been killed. Within the mouth of the canyon he spurred to her side, again shouting his warning.

"Sylvester! Ernie Sylvester!"

She heard. She curbed her racing mount, pulling up as he came to a stop abreast, and for a brief interval the quiet of the night was broken only by the blowing of their winded horses. Then she said in a small voice, "Maybe I shouldn't have done it."

"Burn the stacks? It was a stroke of genius."

"I hate to destroy things." She was terribly serious. "I know what that hay means. It means winter feed. The cattle will starve."

He kneed his horse closer, reaching out and grasping her arm tightly. "It's the one thing that could stop Petry. He won't drive across the sink. He can't afford to. He'll have to drive most of his stock to Elkhead and ship. He won't have cattle to overrun North Mountain, to drive us from our range."

"But our cattle won't have feed either."

They stared at each other in the darkness. Vance Clark took a long breath. "They wouldn't have had feed if Petry had held that hay. We're no worse off for this night's work than he is. Let's get out of here while we can."

He started forward but she reached out and caught his rein.

"Wait," she whispered.

He heard it then: two horses coming fast from above them. He turned his head. Behind them the glow from the distant burning stacks stained the dark sky a kind of crimson. Above them, he was certain, Ernie Sylvester and another rider were coming down, attracted by the light of the fires.

He swung his horse toward the canyon wall, seeking a way upward, a way of escape. The canyonside was very steep, thin brush covering the rock layer which rose like an upthrust crust, cracked and fractured by long forgotten volcanic action to form a rocky ridge high above.

They might have climbed it on foot, but they had no chance on horseback, and both sensed it at once.

"Go on back down the canyon," Clark said. "Make enough noise so they know someone's ahead of them. They won't shoot until they know who it is."

Judy started to protest, but the words died in her throat. She swung her horse and sent him back to the trail, turning downward toward the hot springs.

At once, from the canyon above, a high challenging shout rose to fill the night, and the drum of hoofs came on at a rising pace.

Vance Clark pulled his own mount sidewise, taking advantage of the deeper shadows along the canyon wall. He had no real cover, but he was counting on the sounds of Judy's flight to command the oncoming riders' full attention. In a single motion he stepped from the saddle and jerked his rifle free, laying the barrel across his horse's back as they came around the small turn above him and drove toward the flats.

"Hold up!" He yelled over the din of hoofs.

Without thinking, the startled lead man hauled up and the animal behind drove into the flank of the fore horse. For an instant all was confusion as the riders fought their mounts, and then Ernie Sylvester's high-pitched voice screeched, "Who is it?"

"Clark. Keep your hands in sight or I'll shoot you out of that saddle."

There was a muffled curse. A gun flashed, and the bullet cut the brush a dozen feet above Vance's head. His rifle steadied on the flash, a little below him and to his right. He squeezed the trigger and heard the impact of the bullet even as the high, anguished yell welled up.

The second rider drove his spurs into his horse and dived into the night, the sounds of his passage echoing down the canyon.

Clark quieted his horse with one hand on its neck, locked the reins about a bush and stepped cautiously around it, holding the rifle ready. A horse shifted over to his right, and he paused until he caught a glimpse of the animal as it shied from the shadows across a small patch of moonlight. Its saddle was empty.

He moved in, still cautiously, half expecting a trap. A groan reached him, guiding him back to the rocky trail, and he saw the dark huddled shape that he judged to be a man.

"All right," he said. "Get up."

His only answer was another groan. He risked a match. The flickering flame showed him the contours of Ernie Sylvester's face. Then as the match died he heard a horse coming back up the trail and heard someone call his name.

CHAPTER
SIXTEEN

Vance Clark spun about, his rifle ready. He heard the call again and recognized Judy's voice. Relief flooded over him.

"Here," he said.

She came out of the darkness, pulling her horse to a stop and swinging down near him.

"Who's that?"

"Ernie Sylvester." He bent over the fallen man, lighting a match. The bullet had gone in on the right side, low. Sylvester groaned as Vance leaned down.

"How bad is he?"

Vance's opinion was that the bullet had ranged down into the abdomen, and that the Double M foreman must be bleeding internally, but he did not tell Judy.

Sylvester groaned again and Clark kneeled beside him. Sylvester's voice was weak.

"That you, Shorty?"

"It's Vance."

Sylvester was silent a long time. "You burned the hay fields," he said finally, and drew a labored breath. "That was a smart move. I didn't think you had so much sense."

Vance didn't say anything.

"I saw the glow in the sky." Sylvester seemed to be talking to himself. "I might have known it was you, you damned Indian." There was no rancor in his voice. Any feeling of hostility seemed to have been wiped out by the shooting. He rested a while and then he said, "My side hurts. How bad is it, kid?"

"Pretty bad," Vance said soberly.

"I got a chance?" The voice revealed little besides curiosity.

"Maybe, if you get to a doctor in time."

"You going to get me there?"

"That's up to you."

Listening to Vance Clark, Judy thought she had never heard his voice so coldly expressionless.

Apparently Ernie Sylvester heard it too. He said calmly, "Paying me off, aren't you?"

Vance shrugged in the darkness. "What did you expect?"

Sylvester said, "I misjudged you, kid. I watched you grow up, and I saw you get the breaks from Gil Grover. I figured you were a pretty boy, soft."

Vance let it ride. Sylvester managed a hollow laugh. "I told Bryce Austin that. I told Austin he had nothing to worry about from you. That's a joke on Austin." He laughed again, but it wasn't very convincing.

"There's a man with big ideas." His thoughts seemed to be wandering aimlessly. "He came into this country and he started out to make himself a little king. But his money was good, I'll say that, and he paid promptly."

Vance Clark said, "Is that the reason you shot Gil Grover?"

152

The man on the ground stopped talking. Clark straightened. "Come on, Judy, let's get out of here."

For the first time, Ernie Sylvester sounded worried. "You wouldn't just ride off and leave me?"

"Why not?" Clark moved away. Sylvester tried to sit up, failed and collapsed on the ground. "Don't leave me here to die alone."

"What about Gil Grover? What about Ray Pinker?"

Sylvester seemed to find strength. "Pinker shot him, and that's the truth."

"Pinker said you did."

"You must have had him under the gun. He lied to you. I wasn't within five hundred yards when he cut down. He wanted the gold Austin promised. I was taking it to him when I ran into you at the old mine."

"Will you sign a statement that Austin hired Pinker to kill Gil?"

"Will you take me to the doctor?"

"As soon as you sign."

"Write her out."

Clark searched his pockets for paper and found none. Judy came to his rescue, producing a folded sheet and the stub of a pencil from her pocket. Clark wrote the statement in the light of half a dozen matches, and watched the wounded man sign it.

"See if you can catch his horse, Judy."

The girl stepped into the saddle, freeing her rope, moving off in the half darkness. Sylvester stirred.

"Think I'll make it?"

Clark said, "I hope you last until you can talk to the sheriff."

"You are a cold blooded bastard."

"I've had lessons," Clark said as he turned away. He heard Judy returning and walked toward her. "Find him?"

She nodded. "His reins were dragging." She rode up, leading Sylvester's horse, and sat holding it as Clark lifted the wounded foreman into the saddle and tied him in place. The horse was skittish, not liking his limp burden, but Judy held him with a firm hand.

"Are you going to try to go down by the springs?"

"No," Clark said as he mounted. "We'll ride on up the canyon. There's a track about fifteen miles this side of the ranch which cuts over to the trail." He took the lead rope from her hand and turned up-canyon, Sylvester's horse beside him, Judy following.

They reached the cabin Sylvester had so recently built, and Clark pulled to a halt. "See if you can find some coal oil, Judy."

Judy Grover understood at once. She dismounted, fastened her horse to a tree and disappeared into the building. A few moments later there was a flickering flame which mushroomed into a roaring, leaping fire, outlining her in light as she came from the cabin door.

Sylvester groaned. "You're through, friend Vance."

"You won't be needing the cabin again," Clark said.

"I won't be needing much of anything if we don't hurry. My side feels like it's on fire."

"Think what Grover felt like." Clark started his mount forward, jerking at the lead horse which had a tendency to hold back.

154

They came to the new-strung fence line, and found an ax leaning against one of the pole posts. Clark got down, handed the leap rope to Judy, and used the ax to cut the wire in a dozen places, uprooting the shallow set posts and throwing them to one side.

"I'll haze some cattle down to the springs first chance I get," he said.

They climbed the ridge and dropped into the comparative smoothness of the trail, heading downward again to skirt the sand sink on their way to Elkhead.

False dawn was in the sky before they came to the head of the straggling town's main street and rode down it, pulling to a stop before the frame building which housed the single jail cell and Lem Stewart's living quarters.

The side door was unlocked as usual, and the first intimation the old sheriff had that he was not alone was when he roused to find Vance Clark lighting the lamp on the table.

"Well, well," he said, his old voice made husky by sleep. "I didn't expect you to be obliging enough to come in and give yourself up."

Clark's teeth looked white against the darkness of his face as he grinned mirthlessly. "You'll not live that long, Lem. But I brought you a prisoner in my place. I only hope he's still alive to back up the paper he signed."

The sheriff swung his bare feet to the raw boards of the floor and stood up. He wore an old fashioned night shirt which reached to his ankles and his thin gray hair was all askew. He looked as nearly harmless as a human being can.

"Who'd you bring in?" he inquired.

"Ernie Sylvester."

Lem Stewart had been hiding his emotions for many years, but he showed surprise now.

"How'd you get him?"

"I shot him."

Lem Stewart frowned. "It's still against the law to shoot people in this country, even if some folks do tend to overlook the fact."

For answer Vance pulled the folded paper from his pocket and handed it to Stewart. The sheriff crossed to his desk, searched for his steel rimmed spectacles and read it carefully, twice. When he looked up his face seemed to have aged.

"Have you a witness — I mean someone beside yourself — that Ernie signed this?"

"Judy."

The sheriff ruminated. "She's hardly a disinterested party."

"I'll bring him in. You can have him sign it again in your presence."

"Maybe he's changed his mind."

"He's gut-shot," Vance said, "and he's scared."

He went outside and found Judy waiting beside the lead horse, and Ernie Sylvester slumped in the saddle.

"The doctor," Sylvester said weakly. "Did you get the doctor?"

"Judy will get him." He reached up, loosened the ropes and carried Sylvester into the jail building. He was about to lay him on Stewart's bed when the sheriff

156

objected. "Put him in the cell. I just washed those blankets yesterday."

Ernie Sylvester swore. "A hell of a lot either of you care for a dying man."

Stewart had stuffed his cheek with tobacco while Vance was out. He hit the can in the corner accurately.

"Ernie," he said, "I've known you man and boy for near thirty years, and I disremember one single moment that I ever liked you. When you're standing on two legs you're as ornery a man as I ever knew. And now you've got a slug, which has been coming your way for a long time, you cry like a baby. Dump him in the cell, Vance."

Vance Clark complied.

The sheriff followed them in. He was holding the paper which Vance had given him. "Do you swear that this here is the truth?" he asked the wounded man. "Do you swear that Bryce Austin hired Pinker to shoot Gil Grover?"

Sylvester showed a flash of his old spirit. "Why should I?"

"You want a doctor," Vance said.

Ernie Sylvester cursed him thoroughly. Lem Stewart turned away.

"Let's go, Clark. Maybe he'll be more agreeable in the morning."

"Hey, wait." Sylvester lifted himself painfully. "I'm bleeding to death. I'll swear to anything you want."

The sheriff seemed satisfied. He motioned Vance to follow him, stepping out and closing the door. He locked it, ignoring the wounded man's protest at being left in darkness. Back in his office he shook his head.

"I've seen men shot in the belly, and none of them lasted the way he's lasting."

Clark nodded. "I don't get it. The bullet went into his side. I never expected to get him to town alive."

The sheriff spat at the can. "Well, he's still scared, and as long as he stays scared he's our boy. I think I'll have a talk with the doc before he sees him."

He sat down at the desk, spreading the paper out before him. Then he turned it over. "What is this, Gil's will?"

Vance Clark hadn't realized what it was. He said, "Judy must have been carrying it in her pocket."

The sheriff spoke without lifting his eyes. "Quite a gal you've got there, son."

Vance flushed. "Don't take that will seriously, Lem. That was only Gil's way of making sure I'd stand by the ranch. I'll stick. Judy doesn't have to marry me."

The sheriff looked up. "I'm not much of an authority on marriage, not having indulged in the doubtful pastime myself, but I've observed that people believe in it, especially women. You think she wants to marry someone else?"

"She never said — I don't know —"

"You'd look a long time, and do a lot worse." He broke off as the door opened and Judy came with the sleepy doctor.

The sheriff hoisted himself from his seat at the desk. "Hi, Doc."

Doc Clement nodded. "Hi, Lem."

The sheriff took his arm with one hand, a lamp in the other, and steered him into the short hallway which led to the cell. Judy and Vance looked at each other. The girl sank tiredly into a chair.

"How is he?"

"Who, Ernie?" Vance shrugged. "If you ask me he's too chipper for a man who's going to die. I don't know. He's got a hole in his side."

He broke off as the sheriff came back into the room without the lamp. "Me and Doc had a small talk." Stewart let one old eyelid drop. "Doc ain't going to quiet Ernie's nerves any, no matter what he finds. Him and I have been doing business together for a lot of years." He squinted at them. "You kids could likely use some breakfast."

"Coffee," Judy said in a small voice. "I don't want anything to eat, just coffee."

The sheriff took them into his small kitchen, whistling happily as he prepared bacon and eggs over Judy's protest. He stopped suddenly, in the middle of a note.

"Damn me, I never entertained a woman in my nightshirt before." He almost ran through the door toward the bedroom.

Vance, who had been half asleep, tilted back in his chair and came awake with a start. "What's going on?"

Judy was laughing in spite of her worry and tiredness. "He's a dear."

"Who, Stewart?" It was the first time Vance had ever heard anyone call Lem Stewart a dear.

The sheriff came back in a few minutes, fully clothed, followed by the doctor who demanded hot water and help. "I've got to get the bullet out," he said, opening his bag and beginning to remove his instruments.

"How bad is he?" Judy asked.

The doctor gave her a small grin. "He'll live unless he dies of his own cussedness. The bullet missed his big intestine and struck his hip bone and dug a real nice groove across his back muscles. I've seen worse wounds from a rusty nail."

They gaped at him. "How soon before he finds out he isn't going to die?" the sheriff asked.

The doctor shrugged. "Depends on how smart he is, and how much dope I give him. I'd say maybe a couple of days."

"I wonder," Lem Stewart said slowly, "if that will be long enough to scare Bryce Austin into making his move."

CHAPTER
SEVENTEEN

Bryce Austin liked to sleep late. He had refurnished his room at the hotel at his own expense, even to having the place repapered, and the result was a pleasant, well ordered bachelor establishment.

He opened his eyes, saw the early morning sun slanting in at the east window, and wondered what had awakened him. Then the heavy-handed pounding on the door was renewed and he realized that the battering sound which he had taken as part of a dream was real.

He sat up angrily. "Who's there?"

Petry Munger's rough voice reached him. "Come on, open the door."

Bryce Austin tossed back the covers. He padded across the room in his bare feet and slid back the bolt.

Munger stomped in. His beefy face was a deep, dull red which told louder than any words how very riled he was. Behind him a small man in dusty clothes followed more slowly. Bryce Austin glanced at him, guessed that he was one of Munger's riders, and turned his attention back to the furious owner of the Double M.

"What's happened now?"

"What's happened?" Munger seemed about to explode. "What's happened? That damn Clark fired the hay, that's what's happened. All the winter feed is gone."

Austin frowned, puzzled. "Fired the fields?"

"The stacks. He and someone else rode down on the line camp while the boys were eating. They fired the stacks and when the boys saw the flames and ran out Clark drove them back with his gun."

"Just what will this mean?" Austin asked.

Petry Munger drew a long, tortured breath. "What will it mean? God help me for ever tying up with a stupid son who doesn't even know what it means to lose your winter feed. Well I'll tell you. We won't drive across the sink to North Mountain as we planned. We'll drive to the railroad and ship."

"Where was Ernie Sylvester while all this was happening? You told me Sylvester could handle Clark, that he could handle anything."

"That's another thing." Petry Munger had gotten himself under partial control. "Shorty here was staying up at the new cabin with Ernie. They saw the glow in the sky and they started down to find out what was going on. They heard someone below them in the canyon, and they rode after them. Then a rifle cut loose from the rocks at the side and Ernie went down. Shorty rode on for help. When he got back there with some of the boys Ernie was gone, there was blood on the rocks, the cabin was burned and the new fence was cut." He broke off as if the list of catastrophes was too much.

Austin stared at him in silent contempt. "So everything we started out to do has been stopped, by one man."

Petry Munger sank wearily down on the side of the bed, and Bryce Austin realized for the first time how rapidly the rancher had dressed. He studied him, wondering how he had ever been fool enough to think that he could build Munger into one of the most powerful men in the state. Munger was exactly what the Lord had made him — a stubborn, fighting bully who knew no other way to meet a problem than to lower his head and charge like an enraged bull.

A feeling of deep distaste swept over the lawyer, a distaste for this man, for this country, and for its people. He said, "Get out, Shorty I want to talk to Petry."

The rider retreated through the door as if glad to escape, and Austin turned to the seated man. "All right, Petry. Get a grip on yourself and let's find where we are."

"That's what I've been trying to make out ever since Shorty woke me up," Munger growled. "Sometimes I think I made a mistake ever listening to you. I was doing all right before you came along. Sure, I had a partner, but Gil was too busy with his collections to bother me. He let me run the ranch my way."

Austin said with edged contempt, "But you were ready enough to bolt when I suggested it."

Munger blew out his breath. When he spoke he sounded like a misunderstood child trying to justify its own actions. "Sure, it sounded easy. I thought Gil would jump at a chance to sell. I figured Vance Clark would savvy which side his bread was buttered on and come along. I knew Vance was more than half Indian, but I didn't know one man could give us this much trouble."

Bryce Austin was very tired of hearing about Vance Clark. He said harshly, "The game isn't lost yet, even if you do have to ship your miserable cattle. Clark and the Grover girl are in no better shape. They'll have to ship their stock, too, because they have no more winter feed than you have."

"So how does that help us?"

Bryce Austin checked the sharp retort that sprang to his lips. Although he had very little respect for the beefy man, he still needed him.

"They'll ship," he said. "They'll be paid for the animals, and I'll slap an attachment on the money. Don't forget, I'm suing them in Joetree's name."

"I still don't see where it helps."

Austin lost patience. "You fool. I'll keep the case drawn out in the courts for months, years maybe. Come spring you can buy feeders, but they won't have any money free to restock North Mountain. You can move in then, just as you planned."

Energy flowed back into Munger's big body. His small eyes gleamed. "Couldn't we sue them for burning the hay?"

"If you can prove that Clark did it."

"Three of the crew will swear to that. They're real hostile. They didn't like being shot at. And what about him killing Ernie?"

"So Sylvester's dead?"

Munger nodded emphatically. "You can bank on it. I know Ernie and I know Vance. If they came together, one of them is dead."

"All right," Austin said. "I'll get some clothes on and we'll go to see the sheriff. You get hold of Shorty and any of the rest of the crew if they came into town. Meet me at Stewart's office in half an hour."

Munger had always been a man of action. Inactivity worried him, and he left Austin gladly, his self-confidence almost restored. He headed for his own room on the next floor and was just opening his door when he heard his daughter's voice.

Virginia was standing in her doorway directly across the hall. Her blonde hair was loose, falling in shining abundance about her shoulders, and she wore a blue robe which accentuated her beauty.

"Father, what is it?"

Petry Munger had been unpleasantly surprised that night twenty years ago when his wife presented him with a girl, and surprise still took him every time he looked at his daughter. His wife had been distressingly plain, a hired girl, glad of the chance to marry a range straw-boss, and the idea that any child of his and hers should be the belle of the whole countryside filled him with both a pride, which he did not understand, and an unease, born of the fact that he knew he had very little control over this woman who was his own flesh and blood.

He grew embarrassed, as he always did unless she was fully dressed, and he said, more harshly than he intended, "Nothing, honey. Just a little trouble at the line camp."

"What line camp?"

He had never been too certain of her loyalty, and he said evasively, "The Stinking Water place."

She caught the evasiveness and frowned. "I thought you promised me that you wouldn't have any more trouble with Vance Clark — that you'd let him ride out of the country without being hurt."

His control of his temper slipped. "It's not me that's making trouble with Vance. He burned the hay fields last night and he shot Ernie Sylvester."

Her mouth opened slowly, then closed. "Burned the hay fields? But they belong to us."

He did not answer. He went on into his own room, slamming the door. Virginia stood motionless, prey to a whole range of surging emotions.

She could not quite understand her own reactions. She knew she should be thoroughly angry with Vance. He certainly did not have as much sense as she had always supposed, but on the other hand she did not want him hurt. Her feelings toward him ran back deep into her childhood.

Slowly she returned to her room, uncertain as to what she should do. She finally decided to talk the whole problem out with Bryce Austin. She started to dress, then heard her father leave his room and stomp along the hall. She checked the impulse to call him back, finished dressing and went down to Austin's room.

166

She knocked. There was no answer. She knocked again, then hesitantly turned the knob. The door was not locked and she pushed it open. The room beyond was empty.

At that moment the lawyer was leaving the front door of the hotel. He paused briefly on the porch, looking up and down the nearly deserted street.

It was still early for Elkhead. As in many desert centers, its stores opened late, for most of the customers had a long, time-consuming trip to reach the town.

He came down the steps perfectly poised. He was one of the handsomest men the town had ever known, and without doubt the best dressed.

He wore a black, low crowned hat, the brim rolled; his shirt was white, ruffled and carefully ironed. His only condescensions to the country were high-heeled boots and the cartridge belt about his lean hips, supporting the single light gun.

The gun was a thirty-two, a pearl handled piece with an engraved barrel. Elkhead had been inclined to laugh at that gun when he first arrived, but the laughter had stilled long ago.

Bryce Austin was a perfectionist in everything he did, and he had realized as soon as he had come into the country that Westerners wore guns for use, not for show.

He had always been a good shot, and he proceeded to make himself into a perfect one. He carried a light gun because he hated the weight of a forty-five and the way it pulled the belt down over his hip, and because in

167

his own mind accuracy counted more than the heavy shocking power of a huge hunk of lead.

He saw Munger come out of an early opened saloon, trailed by Shorty and two other riders. He joined them, smelling the rank odor of raw whiskey on Munger's breath.

His contempt for the big man increased, but he kept it out of his voice as he said, "Ready?"

Munger nodded and they made a small parade toward the sheriff's place.

Three people watched them curiously from the far side of the road but they paid no attention. They reached the door which led into Lem Stewart's office. The door was locked, and Petry Munger pounded on it imperiously, first with his big fist and then with the butt of his gun.

The bolt rattled. The door swung inward. The old sheriff glared out at them.

"What's the idea of trying to beat down my door?"

Petry Munger said sourly, "If you were on the job as you should be the door wouldn't have been locked. It's nearly eight o'clock." He stepped in, and the sheriff had to give ground or block his way. Lem Stewart chose to retreat to the old, battered roll-top desk which held all his records. He sank into the creaking chair and surveyed Munger with no pretense of friendliness.

"I suppose you're here on business?"

"You know I never waste time gabbing like you and some of the other old timers. I want to swear out a warrant for Vance Clark's arrest."

"Another?" The sheriff managed to look surprised. "I haven't served the other one yet."

"We didn't think you had," Munger said. "Seems like you're getting a little old for the job, Lem. Maybe next election we can find a younger man."

The sheriff shrugged. "Just as you like, Petry, if you're here to do anything about it."

Munger was startled. "If I'm here?"

"Men don't usually control elections from the penitentiary."

"Penitentiary?"

"It was nice of you to come in here this morning. I haven't served Vance yet, but the warrant against him isn't the only one that's been issued."

He reached into a pigeonhole of his desk and drew out two folded papers. "I've got two warrants here, one for you and one for Austin. You're charged with hiring Ray Pinker, with offering him or anyone else one thousand dollars in gold to murder Gil Grover."

Munger stared at the older man open-mouthed. "Have you gone loco?"

The sheriff ignored this. "I have a statement signed by Ernie Sylvester, swearing that you hired Pinker, that Pinker murdered Gil, that Sylvester was sent up to Joetree's to pay off the thousand in gold, and that when he arrived Pinker was killed accidentally."

The beef color drained from Munger's cheeks, leaving them a curious gray. "I don't believe it."

"Don't believe what?" Lem Stewart's tone had taken on a flinty quality. "Oh, I've got the statement, Petry, all signed and witnessed."

Petry Munger unconsciously dropped his hand to his gun. Behind him, from the doorway which led to the living quarters, Vance Clark said, "Don't try it, Petry. You're covered."

Petry Munger flinched visibly, looked over his shoulder and sagged. Shorty and the other two riders froze fast. Only Bryce Austin seemed unaffected by Vance Clark's sudden appearance. He had made no move for his gun. In fact, he had listened to the sheriff with a slightly amused smile.

"Just where is Sylvester?" he inquired calmly.

"In the cell."

"I'd like to talk to him."

Stewart shook his old head. "Sorry. The doctor says no. The doctor says any excitement might endanger his life." He smiled faintly. "I wouldn't want anything to happen to Ernie, at least not until he testifies at your trial."

CHAPTER
EIGHTEEN

The news that Petry Munger and Bryce Austin had been arrested and accused of having hired Pinker to kill Gil Grover created a sensation in Elkhead. Very few people in the town had liked Petry Munger, but all had feared him, just as all had been impressed by Bryce Austin.

As Vance Clark and Judy moved along the street from the hotel at noon they passed people standing in almost every doorway, discussing the happenings of the morning.

Wild rumors flew about, whereas the truth was that Ernie Sylvester had been moved to the doctor's house and was under guard with a special deputy seated beside his room.

The cell he had occupied now accommodated Petry Munger and Bryce Austin, both of whom found it confining, and both of whom were exceedingly unhappy about the arrangement.

Shorty found himself the temporary ramrod of the Double M crew, a position he neither relished nor understood. The riders had been drifting into town all morning, gathering at the Palace Saloon. Now they were all lined against the bar, discussing their future and the turn of events.

Shorty, who was nearest the window, looked out in time to see Vance Clark on the sidewalk. He had downed half a dozen drinks since the one he had shared with Petry Munger that morning, and they were burning hot and fiery under his belt.

"There's the ranny that caused us all this trouble." He strutted to the door, made brave by liquor and the fact that he had eight men at his back. He burst through the swinging doors as if he had been squeezed from a pastry sack, and then he stopped in the middle of the sidewalk, appalled by the sudden realization that none of the crew had followed him.

Vance Clark did not see him at once. He had been talking to Judy, and the consternation on her face was his first warning. He turned his head away from Judy and found Shorty before him, his gun already in his hand.

Clark stopped. He sized up the small, taut, bowlegged figure, and he sensed that the slightest gesture on his part might make a nervous finger jerk the trigger.

Shorty was not a gunman. In his entire life he had not fired a gun at a fellow man. But now he was trying desperately to build himself up to a killing.

"What's the matter, Clark — afraid to face someone in the daylight?"

Judy stood stock still, gaping at Shorty as if she could not quite believe her senses.

"Shorty," she said.

Shorty did not make the mistake of looking at her. He was steeling himself for the big moment. But he could not squeeze the trigger until Vance Clark made his move, and Vance showed no sign of obliging.

He said levelly, "There are fifty people watching, Shorty. They'll hang you before that gun gets cold."

"Damn you," Shorty said, and he began sweating. "Go for your gun, Clark!"

Vance Clark laughed suddenly. It was the last thing Shorty expected. The idea that a man could laugh at gunpoint was beyond Shorty's comprehension.

He hesitated, half expecting a trick, and in that moment Lem Stewart took a hand in the game. The sheriff stepped from the doorway of the saddle shop behind the short rider, saying in his even, placid voice, "I'll take that gun, Shorty."

Shorty stood like a gnarled statue, hating the knowledge that he had made his play in sight of everyone on the street and had lost. Reluctantly he let his half extended arm droop to his side and the sheriff said, "Take it away from him, Vance."

Vance Clark took the gun from Shorty's unresisting fingers and handed it to Stewart as the old sheriff came up.

"If I had another cell I'd lock you up," Lem Stewart said sternly. "As it is, I'll give you exactly ten minutes to get out of Elkhead and stay out."

"I paid twenty-five dollars for that gun," Shorty mumbled.

"You got cheated," the sheriff told him unfeelingly. "Vamoose." He watched as Shorty ambled back into the saloon, then nodded to Vance and the girl and led the way up the street. When they reached the corner he paused.

"Trouble," he said. "I was coming down to see you at the hotel when I found Shorty playing like a man."

"What now?" Judy said quickly.

"They've applied for bail, and I think the judge will turn them loose."

"But how can he? I thought if you were charged with murder you couldn't get bail?"

The sheriff grunted. "You've got to remember two things," he said mournfully. "First, the judge gets elected, and from where he sits Petry Munger is one of the richest men in the county and Bryce Austin is one of the most powerful men in the state."

"Second, I'm not a lawyer, and the judge may be right. He says the warrant you swore to is faulty. He says the most we can charge them with is being accessories, whatever that is. I guess there's a difference in murderers between the man who pulls the trigger and the man who pays him to do it."

They waited while he shifted his cud to the other cheek.

"And that's not all. The judge went to the jail and talked to Austin. He was saying something about a court order to examine the witness, meaning Ernie Sylvester. Now the doctor has Ernie under dope, but he's going to come out of it sometime, and when he does it's pretty certain that he'll be a mite surprised to find out he's going to live. In fact, if I know Ernie, he'll probably change his story before he gets into court."

"But he was telling the truth," Judy said angrily. "You know that."

"It's not what I know." Lem Stewart said softly. "It's what they manage to pull off in court. Right now it looks like you and Vance hold a winning hand, but frankly I wouldn't give you a plugged quarter for your chances."

"And you uphold the law," Judy fumed. "Somewhere there has to be justice."

The sheriff spat into the dust of the street. "If it'll do you any good I'll take off this badge right now, Judy."

Vance Clark said soberly, "That won't do us any good, Lem, but at least now we know we have a friend at court. Keep us up with what happens."

He took Judy's arm and led her back toward the hotel. He left her in the lobby and climbed slowly toward his room, his mind in turmoil. He reached his door, turned the knob and started in. Then he stopped. Virginia Munger was sitting on his bed.

For an instant he wanted to retreat, but he moved into the room. "You shouldn't be here," he said, closing the door behind him.

She said, "I know it." She stood up, a lithe movement which held a world of grace, and his pulse jumped. "I know it, Vance." She came forward to put a small hand on his arm. "But I had to see you."

He steeled himself against her. "Look, Virginia, we're on different sides of the fence. Let's leave it that way."

"No." She was almost crying. "That's why I'm here. That's what I'm trying to prevent. There's too much between us for any bitterness to break."

The thought came to him that there was too much between them for them ever to be friends again, things which were not of his making, things over which he had no power.

"My father's in jail." She was appealing to him now. "Bryce is in jail. Surely you don't believe either of them had anything to do with Gil's death?"

Silence was her only answer, and she stared at his set jaw with unbelieving eyes. For the first time in her life she had appealed to Vance Clark for understanding and failed to get it.

"Vance, you do believe it."

He said steadily, "It's the truth, Virginia."

She shook her head. "You're bitter because of what has happened."

"It's the truth," he repeated in a steady, dogged undertone. "Believe me, I'd give almost anything I ever hope to own if it wasn't."

She believed him then. He saw it in the sudden darkening of her eyes, the sudden horror in them. "Vance, what am I going to do?"

"Nothing." He had a quick desire to take her into his arms, to comfort her. It was almost irrepressible. He had to fight against it. He held himself utterly rigid. "There's nothing you or anyone else can do."

She was crying, as she had cried when she was a small girl, as she had cried when her least desire had been denied. "I have no right to ask anything of you. I've forfeited that right, haven't I?"

Again silence was her answer.

"But I'm asking anyway." There was deep urgency in her voice. "I'm asking it because you loved me. I'm asking that you don't stand against Father, that you don't stand against Bryce. I know this country. I know that unless you take some action, nothing will happen to them. Promise."

He said, thoroughly miserable, "I can't. I owe too much to Gil. I owe too much to Judy."

"Judy." She flared at him suddenly. "Judy's using you. Judy's always been in love with you and you're too stupid to know it. Judy's twisting you around her finger."

He stood still, shocked. She brushed past him, her breath catching in her throat, and pulled open the door. Judy was just coming along the hall. She stopped, startled, as Virginia burst from the doorway and hurried by, and then she turned back to find Vance in the opening.

For a long minute they looked at each other, and then she started to turn away.

He said "Wait," and the urgency in his voice halted her. "I think you and I had better have a little talk, Judy."

"I'd rather not," she said.

He took a long step toward her and his hand closed about her arm. "I think we'd better."

Reluctantly she let him lead her back into the room and waited until he had closed the door.

"Virginia was here," he said unnecessarily, trying to cover his embarrassment. "She came to tell me that her father and Bryce Austin had had nothing to do with Gil's death."

"And you believed her."

"You know better than that, Judy."

"Vance, I —"

He took both her shoulders in a firm grasp and pulled her forward, forcing her to look up at him.

"Are you in love with me?"

Color came up under the deep tan of her oval face, but she managed a little smile. "What a question to ask a woman."

He said roughly, "Don't go cute on me now. I asked you a fair question. Are you in love with me?"

She stared directly at him. "All right. I am. What about it?"

He let her shoulders go. Of the two he was the less self-possessed. "Why didn't you tell me?"

She was suddenly protective. "Vance. This is a funny world, with funny standards. Women don't tell men. They wait until men tell them."

"But you let me make a fool of myself when we read Gil's will."

She said, "Look, let's be practical." She was striving desperately to be calm. "I knew you were in love with Ginny. I've known it for years, and I also know that you had no chance to get her. What was I supposed to do?"

He could not answer.

"It's a strange world." She sounded a little sad. "I'm in love with you, and you're in love with Virginia, and she's in love with Bryce Austin."

"But —"

178

"Let's forget it," she said matter-of-factly. "I'm glad we had this talk though. In a way it's cleared the air."

He sat down on the edge of the bed, trying to analyze his emotions. He hardly realized that she had disengaged his hands from her shoulders and walked to the door. A moment later she was gone, leaving him with his thoughts. They tormented him.

For the first time in his life he was called upon to compare the two girls. He had known both from childhood and looking back he understood that it had always been Judy who gave way, Virginia whose wishes were fulfilled.

He had never thought about it before, but as his memory ranged across the years he became aware that the younger girl always had stood aside.

He remembered a dozen small injustices which he had not noticed at the time. Like everyone else, he had been hypnotized by Virginia's personality.

He rose abruptly. He had to find Judy. He had to tell her that at last he had stopped being a fool, at last understood what she had gone through all these years. He opened his door and moved along the hall to her room, knocking and then trying the knob. The door was not locked and he thrust it inward.

The room was empty.

He ran down the stairway into the lobby. The lobby too was empty. He crossed it and went outside.

He stopped on the edge of the covered gallery, looking up and down the street. Then he saw Henry

Barlow the harness maker hurrying toward him. The little man paused, breathless.

"Vance, have you heard? Petry and Bryce Austin are out of jail. They're both looking for you."

CHAPTER
NINETEEN

It was very late in the afternoon. The slanting rays of the western sun cast long shadows from the skeleton fronts of Elkhead's warped frame buildings. Usually at this hour the street was fairly crowded with townspeople who, having finished their early supper, sought companionship with their friends along the board sidewalks or in the deep recessed store entrances.

But tonight the street was nearly deserted. Lem Stewart and Vance Clark sat in the sheriff's office, watching the scattered activity with a seemingly careless detachment, neither fooling the other by his apparent lack of interest.

The silence drew long and heavy, and for Lem Stewart, unbearable. "I'd never have believed," he said unhappily, "that I'd be taking sides in a partisan fight. A man with a star is in a funny spot, Vance. He knows everyone and yet he can't have any real friends, not if he does his job thoroughly."

Vance Clark did not answer, and the sheriff eyed him bleakly. "You don't understand that, do you? Your loyalties are clear cut and not complicated."

Vance spoke without turning. "Not entirely."

Lem Stewart said, "No, I suppose not. There's Virginia."

"I wasn't thinking about her," Vance lied. "I was wondering how long Petry and Bryce Austin can stay in that saloon. They have to come out sometime."

Lem Stewart knew that as well as Vance did, and he had been sitting there considering what would happen when they did come out.

Petry Munger had stomped away from the cell breathing threats. That was why Stewart had sent Henry Barlow to warn Vance that the rancher was free. Also, he had warned Petry, speaking more harshly to him than he had ever spoken in his life.

"You won't hunt Vance," he had told him flatly, "and you won't cause any trouble in this town — or, bail or no bail, court order or no court order, you'll go back in that cell and stay there until the fall session of court."

Petry had sneered at him, but Bryce Austin had caught Munger's arm. "Don't waste your time on Stewart. He's not important."

The older man had permitted himself to be led into the street, still muttering threats, and they had disappeared into the Palace Saloon.

They had not reappeared.

They were still in there, with the Double M crew who had been there since morning. The town watched the door, and speculated, and kept away from that part of the street. Lem Stewart sat in his window and watched. From that window he had seen Vance leave the hotel, and he had cursed under his breath as he saw Clark head toward his office. He had hoped that the boy would have sense enough to take Judy and get out of town. But apparently it had never entered Vance's head that it might be wise to retreat.

He had reached Stewart's office half an hour ago, and here they sat.

"I don't suppose," the sheriff said, "it'll do any good for me to advise you to go back to the ranch?"

"Would you, in my shoes?"

Lem Stewart shifted his old bones in the creaking chair. "That's a silly question. Nobody can ever decide what he'd do if he was in another man's shoes because he never is. The things that rowel one fellow don't even tickle the other. The question is, what good can you do here?"

"I won't run."

"Now you're talking like a man with a belly full of pride, and a proud man is usually a foolish one. You know there isn't a man in that saloon who isn't thirsting for your blood, or a person who isn't betting on how many hours you're going to last. So tell me — how are you going to be any help to Judy if you're dead?"

He got no response whatever. He called it quits. "Me, I'm going to get some coffee."

Vance stood up. "That's exactly what I need."

"I didn't mean that," the sheriff said hurriedly. "I'll bring you some."

Vance's lips curved in cold amusement. "Meaning you don't want to walk along the street with me?"

At once the old man was affronted "You know better than that. Petry Munger and Bryce Austin together couldn't keep me holed up in this office like a bear in a tree. Come on."

They moved out toward the hotel, conscious that people watched them from the interior of every store they passed. It was nearly dark now. Lamps were lighted in half the buildings, their flickering yellow flames splitting the gloom, the smell of their burning oil leaking from the open windows to cloud the hot evening air.

They reached the hotel steps and paused by common impulse, glancing back at the saloon across the street, both certain that unseen eyes had marked their passing from behind the dirt-frosted windows.

And the same thought was in both their minds as they continued into the lobby. The whole town might be betting on the outcome of the night, but no one intended to take a hand.

Judy rose from a corner chair. Where she stood, the light from the centerlamp fell faintly, and her small face was in shadow.

"Vance."

He said lightly, "The sheriff and I are going to have some coffee. Interest you?"

She came forward then, and her face was taut and strained. "The whole of Munger's crew are down there, Vance."

"I know it."

"You're going to be killed."

"Not if I can help it."

"I'm going to talk to Petry. I'm going to tell him he can have the ranch." She started for the door. He caught her with three quick strides. His fingers closed on her arm and for a moment they stood facing each other, oblivious of the sheriff, of the watching desk clerk.

He said solidly, "We've got to live with this, Judy. We can't start by ducking something."

Color came up into her cheeks as she understood what he meant, and he went on in a softer tone. "Let me handle this. Trust me."

"I do," she said, and before she realized what he intended he bent his head and kissed her lightly on the lips.

"All right, that coffee is getting cold," he said, and walked past the gaping clerk into the dining room.

Lem Stewart met the clerk's eyes. The man winked. Stewart said harshly, "You can find trouble without hunting it, friend," and left the clerk open-mouthed behind him.

Usually at this time the long dining table was well filled. Tonight there was no one in the big room.

They found seats near the center of the table and an Indian girl came from the kitchen to serve them. Her dark eyes rolled as she looked at Vance, and it was plain to see that she, along with the rest of the hotel kitchen help, considered that they were serving a man already dead.

Judy ordered coffee only, but both men ordered ham steaks and fried potatoes. She watched them eat, shaking her head from time to time, marveling that either had any appetite.

They had almost finished when they heard a disturbance at the door. They turned to see Dr. Clement come into the room. His face was white and the hand which he lifted to wipe across his mouth shook.

"They took him," he said.

Lem Stewart stood up slowly. "Ernie Sylvester?"

The doctor nodded. He was laboring under some emotion which made his voice tremble, and Vance Clark judged that it was anger.

"They came to my office ten minutes ago, by the back door. They knocked out your deputy and carried Sylvester away."

"Carried?"

"I'd given him a hypo. He was — well, you know. Under considerable pain."

Stewart had begun swearing under his breath. "I should have expected something like this, but I didn't figure they'd make any move until full dark. Who were they?"

The doctor shook his head. "I couldn't swear in court. They had their faces masked. But I'd be willing to gamble my last cent it was some of Munger's men."

"Where'd they take Sylvester?"

"I don't know."

Stewart started for the door. Vance Clark went after him, but the old man halted at the entrance. "You keep out of this," he said sharply. "This is strictly my business. It has nothing to do with your fight against Petry or Bryce Austin. Ernie Sylvester was my prisoner. If I need help I can call on any man in town, but if you come with me it'll look like I'm taking your side in a private war."

He stomped out. Vance hesitated.

"He's right," Judy said. "If you go with him it will line him up in our trouble, and that isn't fair to him. Sit down."

Vance obeyed unwillingly. "It's because we brought Ernie down that he's in a tight right now."

"That was the chance Lem took when he ran for sheriff in the first place," she said practically. "He understands that. He didn't want you along."

The doctor sank down into a seat at the far side of the table and used a handkerchief to mop his forehead. "I don't like any of this. Why did Petry have to go and start all this trouble?"

Vance Clark grunted and got up again and left the room, Judy followed him out and across the lobby. He stopped before one of the front windows, and she came up behind him just as he peered out into the rapidly darkening street.

They were in time to see the old sheriff approach the saloon. Just before he entered Lem Stewart paused, looking up and down the wide street. It was almost as if he wanted one last look at the town he had ruled for so long.

Lem Stewart glanced at the hotel and saw Vance's figure outlined by the lobby lights at his back. He smiled ruefully and used the heel of his left hand to kick aside one of the swinging doors.

The room beyond was long, narrow and smoky. To the left were half a dozen tables, and at the largest of these Petry Munger and Bryce Austin sat alone, not talking, watching the Double M crew which was lined up along the bar.

The sour smell of spilled beer and raw whiskey mingled with the smoke, making the old familiar mixture, yet there was something wrong with the whole atmosphere. Out of his long experience Lem Stewart recognized danger at once. The room was dead silent.

Ordinarily with a dozen men drinking the place would have throbbed with the rumble of conversation, punctuated by easy laughter. Tonight there was no laughter. No one talked. No one drank.

They stood waiting, like so many cocked guns set to be released by a common trigger. He knew they had expected his arrival. Or maybe they had expected Vance Clark.

He stopped inside the door, and sensed that the whole scene had been planned, even rehearsed, for not one of the crew turned. Instead they lifted their eyes and watched him in the back-bar mirror.

Bryce Austin and Petry Munger watched him too, not moving, giving no sign of greeting or recognition. Stewart smiled a brief, inward smile. Ignoring the hired hands at the bar, he moved across the rough boards, directly toward the seated men.

He stopped. The silence seemed to increase, as if the gathering held its collective breath. His voice sounded extra loud and harsh in the resulting vacuum.

"I thought you knew me better than that, Petry."

Petry Munger stirred but did not speak.

188

"I didn't expect Austin to understand," Lem Stewart said. "He's new to the country. Things that seem important to us might not impress him. But you, Petry — you knew I'd never sit still when I lost a prisoner. That's all I've got, my pride, and my pride doesn't let me lose a prisoner."

Still Petry Munger curbed his tongue. But nothing held Bryce Austin.

"That pride didn't make you arrest a wanted man." His tone was a gibe. "You've got warrants for Vance Clark's arrest. I don't see you serving them. Instead you walk the street with him as if you were his bodyguard."

The sheriff said dryly, "I run my office my way. Vance Clark will be in court any day I say. Right now I want Ernie Sylvester."

Bryce Austin stared back at him, his eyes bright with malice. "Are you trying to tell me that Ernie Sylvester has escaped?"

"You know he has. But I wouldn't call it escaping. He was at the doctor's house, under guard, and under a sedative. He was carried away."

"Now who do you suppose would do that?"

A murmur of laughter ran along the bar, ending with a loud guffaw. It was the laughter which broke Lem Stewart's iron control. In all his years of wearing a badge no one had ever laughed at him when he was performing his sworn duty.

He said sharply, "Get on your feet."

Bryce Austin did not move. Stewart let his hand drop to the gun at his hip. And then Bryce Austin shot him, the bullet just clearing the table's edge as it slanted up from the 32 which the lawyer had been holding in his lap.

Lem Stewart stood there, an expression of disbelief twisting his face. He made no effort to lift his gun. His arm seemed to lack the strength to lift the big weapon. Then he grasped his stomach with one hand and sat down slowly on the scarred floor. He sat thus for a moment, then fell sidewise in a crumpled heap.

Petry Munger stared down at the fallen man. Then he looked at Austin.

"What did you do that for?"

Austin lifted his gun into sight, examined it casually, and dropped it into his holster. "It was the only way," he murmured.

Anger burst out of Petry Munger. "The only way? You fool, you've turned the town against us."

"Who's going to lead them?" Bryce Austin snapped.

That stopped Munger, and Austin went on. "Stewart was lining up with Vance Clark. You know that, and this thing has dragged out too long. There'll be a new sheriff. I think Shorty would make a good one." He nodded toward the bar where the little range boss stood open-mouthed and dumfounded. "You control the county commissioners. Get them to appoint Shorty tonight."

Munger pawed at his mouth, unable to keep up with Austin's speed and boldness.

"You can't play this game halfway, Petry. It's whole hog or none. Shorty will investigate Stewart's death and they'll decide it was an accident."

190

"The town'll never believe that," Munger mumbled.

"What the town believes is one of my lesser worries. What Vance Clark believes is the chief concern."

He pointed a long finger at the line of men along the bar. They watched him, fascinated.

"I'll pay a thousand dollars gold to the man who gets Clark," he said. "Clark is in town. See that he doesn't get out."

CHAPTER
TWENTY

The shot from the saloon rang through the town like a signal bell. Elkhead's citizens had been waiting for trouble and it alerted them all. But even so, only one man in town heeded the shot as a call to action.

Before the crashing echoes died along the street, Vance Clark headed for the hotel door. But fast as he acted, Judy was faster. She closed both small hands about his arm and she planted her bootheels, dragged against him with her full power.

"Vance, wait."

"Lem needs help."

"There was only one shot," she said desperately. "If he fired it, he's got things under control. If he didn't, you'd just be walking into a room full of armed men waiting to kill you."

He stopped. "I can't just stand here."

"Go out the back door, cut down the alley and come around at the rear of the saloon."

He ran out. She looked after him, anxiety wiping all beauty from her face. Then she remembered the loaded shotgun which the manager always kept behind the hotel desk. She scurried across the room and took the shotgun down from its deer-hoof rack.

"What are you doing?"

Judy turned. Virginia Munger had come part way down the hotel stairs.

"I heard a shot," Virginia said.

"You heard one," Judy's voice was bitter. "Blame your father. Blame that precious lawyer you're going to marry, if he lives through the night."

Virginia's face whitened. "What are you talking about?"

"They've been sitting in the saloon all afternoon, plotting. Then a little while ago they stole Ernie Sylvester from the doctor's house, and Lem Stewart went over there to see them. They shot him."

That really frightened Virginia. "Are you sure?"

Judy was sure. She knew Lem Stewart. If Stewart had still been on his feet he would have walked some prisoners out of the saloon long ago. She said shortly, "I'm sure, but Vance has gone to find out."

"Vance? If there's trouble they'll kill him."

"It's a little late for you to start worrying about that, Ginnie. He'll take care of himself."

"I don't understand you," Virginia wailed. "I never understood you."

"You never tried to understand anyone but yourself. Get back up those stairs and out of the way."

"But I —"

Judy raised the shotgun.

"Get back up those stairs," she said.

Virginia gasped. "I believe you *would* shoot me."

"I'd love to, Ginnie. I just want an excuse."

The older girl retreated, stumbling in her haste. Judy hurried through the dining room and into the kitchen. Ignoring the excited help who were chattering at the serving table, she stepped through the open door into the alley.

Here everything was in deep shadow. She peered first one way and then the other, but did not see Vance. He had already rounded the corner at the cross street and was moving swiftly down its length.

At the signal of the shot most of the storekeepers and many of the householders had blown out their lamps. Long experience with trouble had taught the town that the only safety lay behind barred doors in a darkened house.

Vance Clark welcomed the gloom. The moon had not yet risen, and the side street enveloped him like a trouser pocket. His boots made no sound, for he kept to the dusty middle of the street, avoiding the sidewalk and its hollow-echo boards.

He reached the main street and peered around the corner. The only buildings which still showed lights were the hotel and the saloon. In the saloon lights he saw the group of Double M riders, who had emerged from the building and gathered in a tight knot. They separated, some heading toward the hotel, others toward the foot of the street. He could tell by their actions that they were hunting, and he did not have to guess at the quarry.

He waited in the darkness, but the three who had come up the street went into the hotel.

194

He knew now that the sheriff had to be dead, but he wanted to make sure. He took a chance, ducking across the main street and into the shadows of the cross street beyond.

Once within its mouth he moved quickly to the alley and hurried through it. Its narrow length bordered the back yards of a dozen stores. At the saloon yard he turned, cutting across the battered, sunbaked earth, littered here and there by small piles of rusty cans.

He avoided these and reached the rear door without sound. He rested long enough to recover his breath, then pushed the door open.

For a moment he thought the long room was empty except for the single bartender, but then he saw Petry Munger slumped at a table against the far wall, and the sprawled figure of Lem Stewart on the splintered wooden floor in front of Munger.

He had known that the sheriff must be dead, but the actual sight of the old man filled him with a cold, killing rage. He pushed the door wider and stepped inside.

"Petry," he said.

Petry Munger had been sitting at the table in a kind of daze. For the first time in his arrogant life he realized that things had gotten out of his control, that Bryce Austin, not he, was the real boss. Any doubt of that had vanished as he watched his crew throng out into the street in response to Austin's order.

He lifted his eyes now, and for an instant failed to recognize the man who stood beside the rear door. The big ceiling lamp hung between him and Vance Clark, and it half blinded him. Then he realized who it was, and for the first time in his life real panic hit him.

It was fear, not reason, which lifted him out of his seat, fear based on guilt which sent his hand sweeping down toward his holstered gun.

The movement caught Vance Clark by surprise. He had known Petry Munger since his early boyhood, and at one time he had expected to marry Munger's daughter. He had understood when he stepped into the saloon that the clash was inevitable, but he had imagined words first, bitter words, recriminations. He could not know that Munger's conscience, suddenly laid bare, would force the big man into instant action.

He saw Munger's fingers close around the smooth stock, saw the gun actually start to rise from its bed in the holster before he made his own move.

His shot came a split second after Munger's, but the timing was so close that to the shock-stunned bartender the blast of the two guns seemed to blend into one roar. Munger's hurried shot dug into the rough boards at Vance's feet. He never fired a second, for Vance's bullet caught him directly in the heart. He fell, his big body collapsing, almost obscuring that of the old sheriff.

Vance never gave him a second look. Echoing the shots, a high yell rode up from the street outside the saloon, and rushing feet scuffed along the boardwalk. He ducked back into the rear yard, his smoking gun still in his hand. He hesitated in the alley, trying to decide which way to go. Behind him feet hammered across the saloon floor. A man appeared in the doorway

196

he had just left, and a shot split the night, the bullet whining inches from Vance's head.

He fired in return and drew a high, startled yell. He swung away, sprinting down the alley as best he could in his high-heeled riding boots. He covered less than half the distance and then a shadow rose in the alley's mouth and a bullet tugged at his sleeve.

He flung himself to the left, dodging into the yard of a general store, crossing its littered surface and finding an unlocked rear door. He slid into the darkness beyond and his nerves jerked and quivered as a woman let out a shrill scream. After that a quavering male voice came through the blackness.

"Who is it?"

He waited until his heart stopped hammering so wildly. Then he said, "Vance Clark. They just shot the sheriff."

The silence which greeted him was more eloquent than any words. No one in Elkhead was better known than Lem Stewart, and no one more respected.

Finally the woman said, "Get out of here. This isn't our fight. If they find you here they'll kill us."

Clark thought grimly that if he started back out through the littered yard there would be no doubt of it. He would be dead.

The man said, "Where's Petry Munger? I'll talk to him. He'll listen to me —"

"He's dead," Vance Clark said flatly, and silence descended again.

It was broken by a sudden pounding on the rear door.

Vance stiffened, the gun in his hand seeming to increase in weight as he tightened his grip. Upon entering and closing the door he had automatically slid the thick bolt into place, and he thanked his lucky stars for the unconscious action.

The pounding grew louder and a harsh voice said, "Come on, Clark, open up. We know you're in there."

The man behind Clark breathed noisily, trying to speak in a calm, unhurried tone. "There's no one here but me and my wife."

For an instant the yard was quiet. Then came a muttered conference, and the harsh voice again.

"All right, open up. We'll have a look."

In the darkness Vance Clark found the storekeeper's arm. He gripped it hard. "Tell your wife to get down behind something," he whispered. "Then open the door."

The man began to tremble. Clark increased his pressure on the arm. "Do as I say," he hissed, and his words were covered by the insistent pounding.

He felt the man move forward. He released his grip, and shifted position so he would be standing behind the door as it swung inward.

The storekeeper fumbled with the bolt in the dark room, saying in his worried voice, "Hold on, hold on. I'm trying to open it."

The bolt scraped and clicked. The door was thrust in so violently that it almost knocked the storekeeper backward. He stumbled over something and fell flat, whether by design or accident Vance had no way of knowing. He had a moment to be thankful that the man was relatively safe, and then one of the Double M riders was standing beside the open door, scratching a match with his free hand, his gun in the other.

The match flared only once before it sputtered and died, but it located the man's head nicely. Vance Clark swung his gun down fast and the heavy barrel chunked against bone and the body thumped on the floor.

Outside, in the dark yard, a voice yelled, "Slim, Slim, are you all right?"

Vance fired at the sound, and heard the thud as his slug struck flesh. He heard the man groan as he fell and he bulled ahead into the darkness.

His toe struck something soft. He stumbled. He saved himself from falling only by trampling the prostrate man, and then he was running free along the alley length, conscious of shouts which echoed through the town.

Apparently there had been only two Double M riders behind the store, but he had little time to congratulate himself. The town was alive with Munger's men. Every shadow might hide an enemy. Each building corner he turned might burst into flaming death.

CHAPTER
TWENTY-ONE

Judy came back in through the hotel kitchen, crossed the dining room and entered the lobby. She was still carrying the shotgun which she had taken from the wall behind the hotel desk. She stood undecided for a moment, then hurried to the front window.

She got there in time to see the knot of Double M riders in front of the saloon break up into two groups, the larger one moving up the street toward the hotel.

With no time to spare, she placed the shotgun in the corner behind a leather backed chair, then stationed herself in the middle of the long room. The tramp of boots shook the gallery steps. She had never felt so alone in her life.

She steeled herself to face them, but it came as a distinct shock when Bryce Austin walked through the door. She could have coped with Petry Munger or any member of his crew, but at sight of the lawyer she lost control. She hated him as she had never hated any other human being. All of the trouble which had engulfed everything she held dear had been created by this . . . this . . .

"What do you want?" she fairly shouted at him.

200

Bryce Austin had two men with him. They hung back a little, but the lawyer seemed to derive pleasure from her obvious rage.

"Where's Clark?" he asked, smiling thinly.

"He's not here!"

"He hasn't left town, my dear. He's probably hiding somewhere in this hotel."

Caution bade her remain quiet, but pride would not let her. "Vance never hid from anyone in his life — certainly not from you."

Austin jerked his head toward the stairs. "See if he's up there."

The two cowboys edged around Judy, made uneasy by her open contempt. The first man reached the bottom of the steps, and a shot rang out from across the street.

Bryce Austin swore and ran to the front window. Through it he saw several Double M riders converging on the saloon they had just left.

"Never mind searching upstairs," he called to his two men. "Watch the girl." Then he bolted outside, slamming the door behind him.

From her place near the windows Judy saw him dash down the porch steps and run across the street. He paused at the saloon door, probably asking questions. Then he pressed through the cluster of Double M riders and went inside.

He was gone for what seemed to be an eternity. He reappeared in the reflected lights from the saloon windows, standing tall and powerful, his feet wide apart, every movement he made an angry one.

The riders around him scattered the length of the street while he held his place before the saloon like a general directing the operations of a scouting force.

Silence settled across the town, a silence which was broken by a high yell and a burst of shots. The street before Judy leaped into quick focus as the Double M men ran back toward Scarworth's store.

She waited. It was the hardest, longest wait she could recall, and it lasted only a few minutes.

The two men who had been left to watch her were as nervous as cats. One of them moved toward the front windows for a better view of the street. The other fidgeted, then followed.

Judy bolted for the dining room door. They caught her before she reached it, and dragged her back toward the windows, struggling between them.

And then she saw Bryce Austin coming back across the street, trailed by three of his men, and it seemed to her that this must be the end.

She steeled herself not to show her deep emotion, vowing grimly in her heart that she would not stop, that as long as she lived she would carry on the fight.

But through the haze of her own emotions she realized as soon as the lawyer strode into the room that he had none of the elation of victory. His handsome face was flushed and his eyes angry, and it came to her that there could be only one explanation for his rage. Vance had somehow escaped. Vance was still alive.

Relief made her a little dizzy, but it also broke that paralyzing numbness. She shook free from the men who held her and faced Austin.

202

"So your hired killers didn't get him?"

The restraint under which Bryce Austin usually held himself gave way with the explosive quality of a shattered dam. He swore at her. He railed, his words hardly coherent. But out of the jumble she picked the fact that Petry Munger was dead.

She felt no exultation. She cared only that her guess had been correct. Vance had escaped.

"You'll never catch him!" The words burst out of her.

They stopped Bryce Austin's tirade. He paused, filling his lungs with air as if meaning to start again, but when he spoke it was in a quiet, controlled voice.

"Maybe you'll help us. Apparently Clark's in this fight for you. He's killed Petry and wounded a couple of my men. He's still in town and he can't get out because I've got riders watching. Come on, walk down the main street with me."

She stared at him.

"He'll see you," the lawyer said, "and if I know Clark he'll want to know what I intend doing with you, and he'll come out to find out."

She said, "I'm not going," and walked to a chair and sat down.

Bryce Austin grinned, wolfish. He gestured to the two guards. "Pick her up. Carry her out. Be as rough as you have to. The louder she yells the sooner Clark will show himself."

They hesitated, looking foolishly at each other.

"Do as I say, damn it!"

Both started to advance on Judy, but they moved gingerly, as if they might be attacking a mountain lion.

Judy got up. "I'll walk," she said, and moved toward the door.

Vance Clark saw her as she came out. She paused at the top of the hotel steps, and he saw Austin and the Double M riders behind her.

He was across the street in a narrow passage between the blacksmith shop and the saddler's, a passage so narrow that there was hardly room for the width of his shoulders between the rough walls. He had been trying to get back across the street, but the return of Austin and his men to the hotel had caused a delay.

If he could recross without being seen, he might manage to work down the alley toward the livery stable. He had been about to attempt a dash for it when Judy appeared.

He crouched, still concealed in the shadows, blaming her for foolhardiness in showing herself. Then he realized that she was not acting under her own volition. She was being forced by the men around her.

He cursed Bryce Austin silently. He knew what Austin intended. He should have expected just such an action from the man. If Judy should be killed in the cross-fire of the street it would simplify Austin's effort to control the country, and it could be called an accident.

They moved down the street, Judy in front, the five Double M riders fanned out behind her, one on each sidewalk, and Bryce Austin bringing up the rear.

It was a trap, a trap well baited, death stalking down the street. Austin was falling farther and farther behind his men as if to assure his own protection.

They passed the shadowed opening where Vance crouched, never once glancing into the dark cavity. It was too close to the store where the last shooting had occurred, too close to the saloon where Petry Munger had died. It never entered their minds that Clark would be fool enough to stay so near.

But Judy understood Vance far better than they did. Her fear was not that he might try to escape, but that he would be rash enough to face these men alone.

She had hardly passed his hiding place before she raised her cry. "Vance, Vance, keep back! It's a trap!"

The rider walking directly behind her cursed violently and grabbed her arm, twisting it until he forced her to her knees, but she made no further sound.

Vance had all he could do to restrain his impulse to leap forward into the roadway. But he held himself, because if he moved now he would come between the men guarding Judy and Bryce Austin.

He watched them go by. Judy was in the middle of the street, one man with her, the others now on the sidewalks a dozen steps behind her. Farther back Bryce held the street center, his boots stirring up little swirls of dust with each step.

He passed Clark and traveled some fifty feet onward. Vance decided to make his move. Judy was well beyond Austin, as nearly out of harm's way as was possible under the circumstances. At least she would not be in the crossfire.

He moved into the open, silent as one of the shadows from which he came. He was relaxed, unhurried, making no sound until he was entirely clear of the buildings, out in the street with a clean view of both boardwalks.

"Judy — drop!"

The shout racketed among the buildings, and the Double M men, made tense by their own dark thoughts, did not immediately detect the direction from which it came.

But Judy reacted at once. She went down to her hands and knees and scrambled toward the hitching rail which fenced the right hand sidewalk.

Bryce Austin's hand had flown to his gun at the first sound of Vance's voice. He pulled the weapon, looking around wildly for something to shoot at.

"Back here," Vance Clark said.

Austin swung and snapped a wild, high shot at the man he had been hunting. His second shot was lower. It whispered wickedly past Vance Clark's shoulder.

And then Vance's first bullet struck Austin in the throat.

One of the men from the left sidewalk threw a bullet at Clark. The heavy slug hit him in the side, knocking him from his feet.

The shot, which might have killed him, saved his life. He was down in the dust, and the barrage of bullets which the five riders poured at him cut nothing but the air above his prostrate body.

They, and Judy, and the townspeople watching from their darkened windows thought he was dead. He was hurt, but not so badly so that he lost his senses. His right hand still held his gun, and he gathered his remaining strength, lifting himself on his left elbow.

206

Then, coolly, deliberately measuring the shots, he began firing.

His first two bullets dropped two men, one coming from each side of the street. The others turned and ran, the guns in their hands empty from their excited shooting.

And Judy had jumped to her feet. She came racing back. She paused for an instant beside Bryce Austin's body, snatched up his fallen gun, and snapped off two shots to hasten the retreat of the Double M men.

The street was theirs, Clark still down in the dust, resting on his elbow, his gun still held ready. Townsmen who for twenty years would tell and retell the story of this fight came slowly from their hiding places, sensing with the instinct of their kind that the battle was over.

Petry Munger was dead. Bryce Austin lay twisted grotesquely in the dust. The crew they had hired felt no loyalty to a lost cause. They were gunmen, fighting for pay, and the wallets which had paid them were flat forever. Those who still lived would have but one thought — to get out of the country as quickly as they could.

The crowd gathered, talking excitedly, and Doc Clement came to bend over Vance, shaking his head as he examined the groove that the heavy slug had cut, the rib it had broken with its shocking power.

Clark was up on his feet, insisting that he could walk, supported by two volunteers, when he saw Virginia come slowly through the crowd. She refused to look at him as she passed. She moved on to stand with bowed head beside Bryce Austin.

Clark felt sorry for her, but that was all. Remorse did not touch him, nor did he have any sense of loss. A job which had needed doing was now complete, and a chapter in his life had ended.

He turned, and found Judy watching him with a kind of quiet torment in her eyes. He smiled to reassure her. He took a step toward her, not knowing how weak he was, and stumbled. He felt the hands on his arms tighten to support him, and he had just enough strength left to say, "It's all over, Judy. All finished."

Her smile told him that she understood, and he let the men lead him away to the doctor's office, knowing that she followed, knowing that everything was going to be all right.

About The Author

Todhunter Ballard was born in Cleveland, Ohio. He was graduated with a Bachelor's degree from Wilmington College in Ohio, having majored in mechanical engineering. His early years were spent working as an engineer before he began writing fiction for the magazine market. As W. T. Ballard he was one of the regular contributors to *Black Mask Magazine* along with Dashiell Hammett and Erle Stanley Gardner. Although Ballard published his first Western story in *Cowboy Stories* in 1936, the same year he married Phoebe Dwiggins, it wasn't until *Two-Edged Vengeance* (1951) that he produced his first Western novel. Ballard later claimed that Phoebe, following their marriage, had co-written most of his fiction with him, and perhaps this explains, in part, his memorable female characters. Ballard's Golden Age as a Western author came in the 1950s and extended to the early 1970s. *Incident at Sun Mountain* (1952), *West of Quarantine* (1953), and *High Iron* (1953) are among his finest early historical titles, published by Houghton Mifflin. After numerous traditional Westerns for various publishers, Ballard returned to the historical novel in *Gold in California!* (1965) which earned him a Golden Spur Award from the Western Writers of America. It is a story set during the Gold Rush era of the 'Forty-Niners. However, an even more panoramic view of that same era is to be found in Ballard's *magnum opus*, *The Californian* (1971), with its contrasts between the *Californios* and the emigrant gold-seekers, and the building of a freight line to compete with Wells Fargo. It was in his historical fiction that Ballard made full use of his background in engineering combined with exhaustive historical research. However, these novels are also character-driven, gripping a reader from first page to last with their inherent drama and the spirit of adventure so true of those times.

ISIS publish a wide range of books in large print, from fiction to biography. Any suggestions for books you would like to see in large print or audio are always welcome. Please send to the Editorial Department at:

ISIS Publishing Limited
7 Centremead
Osney Mead
Oxford OX2 0ES

A full list of titles is available free of charge from:

Ulverscroft Large Print Books Limited

(UK)
The Green
Bradgate Road, Anstey
Leicester LE7 7FU
Tel: (0116) 236 4325

(Australia)
P.O. Box 314
St Leonards
NSW 1590
Tel: (02) 9436 2622

(USA)
P.O. Box 1230
West Seneca
N.Y. 14224-1230
Tel: (716) 674 4270

(Canada)
P.O. Box 80038
Burlington
Ontario L7L 6B1
Tel: (905) 637 8734

(New Zealand)
P.O. Box 456
Feilding
Tel: (06) 323 6828

Details of **ISIS** complete and unabridged audio books are also available from these offices. Alternatively, contact your local library for details of their collection of **ISIS** large print and unabridged audio books.